Tales from
LITTERDALE

John Morrison

Halsgrove

First published by Halsgrove in 2002

British Library Cataloguing-in-Publication Data
A CIP record for this title is available from the British Library

ISBN 1 84114 215 8

HALSGROVE
Halsgrove House
Lower Moor Way
Tiverton EX16 6SS
T: 01884 243242
F: 01884 243325
www.halsgrove.com

Printed in Great Britain by
The Cromwell Press, Trowbridge

ACKNOWLEDGEMENT

These articles are adapted from those which first appeared in *Peak & Pennine* and *Peak District Magazine*, published by Dalesman Ltd.

INTRODUCTION

LITTERDALE DISCOVERED
By Roly Smith

I suppose I should be held responsible for launching John Morrison's hilarious Peakland village of Litterdale on an unsuspecting public. As the founding editor of the monthly magazine *Peak & Pennine*, which was published by Dalesman for two years from June, 1997 (it is now known as *Peak District Magazine*), I was looking for a writer who could raise a smile among our fast-growing army of readers. I knew just how difficult it was to sustain this kind of writing, having contributed a similar light-hearted, satirical column to a leading outdoor magazine for two years myself.

I had come to know John chiefly as an outstanding landscape photographer, especially of his home ground, the Yorkshire Dales. But I also knew John as an acerbic wit, who had written some very funny and successful books about life in a small, South Pennine milltown. These thinly-disguised portraits of his adopted home of Hebden Bridge so upset the local newspapers that any mention of the books was banned from their pages. As John pointed out: "It was the best publicity I could have had."

The first "Tales from Litterdale" column appeared in April 1998, and I'm pleased to say it's still running. Thousands of readers have been enthralled by the antics of Scoop, the editor of the *Litterdale Times*, stabbing one-fingered at his ancient Remington like a demented woodpecker; Mandy, Litterdale's New Age seer and expert in feng shui, the Chinese art of rearranging the furniture, and busy-body Violet, the self-appointed village guardian and eco-warrior. Then there's Norman, the saintly odd-job man and Bob, the tuneless postman. Bill, the village's tourism officer, hopes his new slogan "Lovely Litterdale: where the present meets the past and makes an elegant swallow dive into the future" is sufficiently bland and meaningless to attract visitors in droves.

The reason that these apparently over-the-top characters work under John's skilful treatment is because if you've ever lived in a village, they will remind you of someone. Their brilliance lies in the fact that they are not too outrageous as to be instantly recognisable, because every village, indeed every community, has a Mandy, Voilet, Norman, or Bob.

The real star of these tales, though, is the village itself. I'm reliably informed that Litterdale lies smack in the middle of the Peak District National Park. But don't try to find it on the map. As John points out, the village shares a common border with Fantasia and Never Never Land. But despite being a peaceful backwater, Litterdale has not remained untouched by great events: the millennium, foot and mouth diease, global warming and the exorbitant price of replica football strips.

As Bill once said in one of his deathless slogans, Litterdale is probably closer than you think.

SPRING

There's a price to pay for living somewhere as agreeable as Litterdale. It's one of the Peak's 'honeypot' villages, so we get more than our fair share of visitors. Once we've bade farewell to those long winter days, and seen the little rash of snowdrops appear on the verges of the village green, the more optimistic residents can convince themselves that Spring is finally here.

It's difficult to know why Litterdale is so popular with visitors, rather than any one of a dozen, equally characterful, villages in the Peak District National Park. We wonder which came first: the visitors or the car-park. Certainly, when people find the prospect of ploughing through the pile of Sunday papers just too intimidating, and thoughts turn instead to a day in the country, the cry of 'Let's go to Litterdale' seems to have the alliterative allure that will propel couch potatoes off their sofas and into their cars.

On sunny weekends the traffic snakes sedately towards Litterdale, at the sort of speed that gives our local hedgehogs a better than even chance of getting across the road unsquashed. Visitors are an uncomplaining lot; an hour spent in a traffic jam – with radiators, frazzled parents and fidgety kids all ready to explode – seems to be an essential ingredient of a good day out.

It's one of life's minor mysteries why 'pay & display' car-parks are such an irresistible draw to jaded townies. They want to get away to the country – and Litterdale is surrounded by some of the finest countryside in the White Peak – yet no sooner have they reached a 'pay & display' car-park than their courage fails them. Suddenly they become acutely aware of the umbilical cord that binds them, albeit invisibly, to their cars.

Being a keen walker it's hard for me to understand why so many visitors prefer to mooch around honeypot villages, instead of heading for the hills. The reason, as I was told by a National Park volunteer who leads guided walks, is that a lot of visitors are afraid they'll get lost and not be able to find their way back to their cars. It seems a shame, since escaping the crowds and losing yourself in the landscape is surely one of life's keenest pleasures. And the ability to read an Ordnance Survey map can be learned in a couple of hours by anyone able to decipher the cooking instructions on a four-seasons pizza.

So a lot of visitors will settle, instead, on whatever attractions can be found within 200 yards of the car-park. Perhaps *this* is what makes people descend on Litterdale in such numbers; whatever we've got by way of tourist attractions can be viewed without breaking sweat, or straying far from the comforting presence of the car. So what *have* we got to keep visitors amused (and fractious children quiet) for a couple of hours?

Well, we've got gift shops. A strange concept, gifts; the sort of useless tat you buy for other people, but you wouldn't really thank them for giving to you. There's a sign in one of Litterdale's craft shops inviting visitors to 'meet the craftsmen'. To judge from most of the stock on sale, 'meeting the craftsmen' would presumably entail buying a return air ticket to Taiwan.

Nevertheless, some items are genuinely made in Litterdale. Wonky hand-thrown pottery, for example. The quality control manager of your average Taiwanese sweat-shop would probably have his job on the line if he were to allow such deformed offerings to leave the premises. Even labelling them 'seconds' would invite comment from a Trade Descriptions Officer. The thought occurs: why don't the talentless potters of Litterdale just cut out the middleman, and toss their mis-shapen creations straight into a rubbish skip?

We've got an outdoor shop, called 'Take a Hike'. Perhaps it feels more authentic to buy your fleecy jacket or weather-proof cagoule somewhere rural like Litterdale, instead of in town. All I know is that there are villages where you can't even buy a loaf of bread or a carton of milk any more, but where you'll have no trouble finding a selection of two-man tents or three-season, duck-down sleeping bags.

There was a time – it seems so long ago – when walking was a very simple activity. You'd just slip on something shapeless and warm, and put one foot in front of the other. Now, of course, we scorn such a miserly approach. We're happy to spend folding money to ensure that we look the part. We used to buy a pair of boots or a rucksack; now we buy 'a system'. We used to pull on a mud-coloured windjammer, made from the same low-tech, rain-attracting material from which they make bath sponges. Now we have smart, figure-hugging garments – in this year's tastefully co-ordinated colours, of course – which keep us striding through torrential rain long after the enjoyment has gone... just to see if a £250 cagoule really is as waterproof as the manufacturers suggest.

We used to find a forked stick and whittle it with a pen-knife. It was something to do while waiting in some blighted camp-site for the kettle to boil. The result – after only a few hours of graft, and a couple of bandaged fingers – was a home-made walking-stick. Now we go to an outdoor shop instead and pick up a telescopic pole in lightweight titanium, with three sections and an ergonomic handle. And we spurn something as simple as a penknife, in favour of a Swiss army knife. Isn't it somehow typical of the Swiss that their army should be famous, not for a successful military campaign, but for precision-made cutlery?

You can still buy a Swiss army knife with just a couple of blades, but only a skinflint would be content with that. At 'Take a Hike' the knives recline seductively in a display case. Like the brazen denizens of some red-light district, the pleasures become more exotic with every fiver you're prepared to pay: corkscrew, saw, screwdriver, magnifying glass and that pointy thing that no-one knows what to do with. Towards the top of the range – it's serious 'three-in-a-waterbed' money now – you get a watch, compass, hedge trimmer, arc-welder and full internet connection... plus a smart leather case on wheels to keep it in. You want one. You know you do. But if you have to ask the price, you really can't afford one.

'Fashion on the fells' is what it's all about these days. Having spent years making durable, hard-wearing outdoor clothing in muted colours that wouldn't turn heads or scare wildlife away, the designers and manufacturers are wising up. Now they try to instil a sense of paranoia in ramblers by adding another injunction to the Country Code: You must not be seen walking in last year's colours. The ladies in Litterdale's Tourist Information Centre have a choice expression to describe those couples who arrive in identical – and suspiciously clean – designer walking outfits. 'All the gear and no idea', they say, rather sniffily.

Litterdale has tea-shops, too. Weary from their valiant attempts at Litterdale's own 'Munros' (the aim is to browse around every single craft-shop before acute tannin deprivation sets in), visitors can rest their weary legs and enjoy the restorative effects of tea. Anybody too knackered to lift a cup to parched lips can have it intravenously.

The walls are plastered with pastoral prints, and the place-mats feature hunting scenes; vicarious glimpses of a vanished rural arcadia for those with no intention of feeling anything but Tarmacadam beneath their feet. After a few platefuls of pikelets, tea-cakes, fruit-scones, rum-butter, clotted cream, fancy cakes and – sensibly – some low-calorie cola to wash it all down with, our less adventurous visitors justifiably feel they've enjoyed everything that lovely Litterdale has to offer.

Unseasonably warm spring weather is making Litterdale bloom with flowers. The first swallows are here, recuperating after their long flight north. The trees, still only half in leaf, are full of newly-arrived songbirds. The willow warbler's cadence evokes the summer days to come almost as vividly as the sighting of the first ice cream van. As he hurtles round another blind bend on two wheels, the ice cream man activates his chime. It is Greensleeves, played on what sounds like a Rolf Harris Stylophone and then blasted out at migraine-inducing volume to the blameless folk of Litterdale. And if the ice cream man is on his rounds, a new cricket season can't be far behind.

It's the shortest of strolls down to Litterdale's cricket pitch, where the team has reassembled after the winter sabbatical. The cricket ground is a reclaimed swamp down by the river: the natural habitat only of flannelled fools, vindictive horseflies and a handful of undemanding spectators with time on their hands.

With water so close a lofted shot to leg is the cue for a young lad to leap, with practised ease, into a canoe conveniently tethered at the river-bank. He paddles towards the ball, fishes it out, paddles back, ties up, gets out, hurls the ball arrow-straight into the wicket-keeper's gloves, and settles back into his deck-chair… as if this was an everyday occurrence. Which it is.

It seems a long time since October, when Dennis, our captain, offered his resignation – as he has done at season's end for the last twenty years. Mortified by presiding over lacklustre performances, and sickened by the smell of the horse liniment with which his ageing team members insist on daubing themselves, he vowed then that he'd played his last game for Litterdale.

But winter has wiped away those feelings of failure that smarted so much at the time. Now that Spring is here he's having a change of heart: 'Maybe just one more season,' he convinces himself. Perhaps this year we are finally going to fulfil our obvious cricketing potential, and not continue to be the talent-free embarrassments we've been for as long as anyone can remember. Or perhaps not.

Spring is, after all, a time of optimism, before unrealistic hopes have been sacrificed at the altar of bitter experience.

I love the game. Cricket, unlike just about everything else that life can offer, has never let me down. It has never ended a potentially rewarding relationship with a mendacious platitude like: 'It's not you, it's me... I just need more space'. Cricket has never borrowed money and then neglected to pay it back. Cricket has never made silver-tongued promises that subsequently turned to ashes.

Once you start to think deeply about the game (and it's designed to be slow and boring, for this very purpose) cricket offers some distinctly uncomfortable home truths. *Beyond* the boundary there are many flags, many allegiances, many contradictory codes of conduct. But *inside* that boundary the two teams conform to a single set of rules, without which the the game has no meaning. And, speaking as a life-long Labour supporter, it comes as quite a shock to realise that a team operates best when presided over by a benign dictator like Dennis. These are the kind of thoughts that pop into your mind, unbidden, when you're fielding down at fine leg with only horse-flies for company.

The air is filled with the sounds of the summer game: mostly screams of pain as a hard leather ball ruptures tender, unprotected flesh. Our batsmen do their best to minimise the potential damage, with Neoprene, bandages, extra sweaters, box, thigh guard and forearm protector. One or two brave souls don helmets; brave because the other players' cruel taunts probably hurt more than a glancing blow to the temple.

When a bowler *does* hit a batsman on the head, it's considered sporting to feign concern for his welfare, ask if he's okay, then stride back way beyond his bowling mark and try to bowl the same ball again. Only faster. It's hardly any wonder that the bowlers' habitual complaint is: 'Umpire, the batsman's gone out of shape.'

The league umpires – small, dapper, pipe-smoking men well into their anecdotage – are kept in a shed during the week. Every

Saturday the team captains come and take their pick, slipping the nominal umpiring fee discreetly into the breast pocket of an immaculate blazer.

There's not a lot to choose between one Brylcreemed umpire and another. They all played cricket in their youth and, through the distorting lens of time, are convinced that the players of today aren't fit to lace the boots of the cricketers *they* knew. If the umpires had a motto it would be: 'The older I get, the better I was'.

After the game the team gravitates towards the pub. The landlord of the Fox doesn't bother to disguise his sneer when he asks them how they've done. He can spot a bunch of losers from a thousand paces. But after a few pints of cooking bitter, the players tend to forget just how soundly they've been beaten. The team's performance will, in beery retrospect, be awarded a heroic perspective that was entirely lacking on the pitch. Yes, the unwarranted optimism of third-rate cricketers is surely a lesson to us all.

SUMMER

A recent poll indicates that commuters would rather spend two hours in stationary traffic than even consider giving up their car and using public transport instead. The mere thought of sitting on the top deck of a bus, surrounded by hacking smokers and old folk rabbiting on about the war, fills the average motorist with a nameless dread.

Never mind that another recent survey indicates that London traffic now moves at an average speed of just 12mph: a stately sort of progress that even the Hansom cab drivers of Victorian times would have considered dilatory. Never mind that we are slowly choking to death on our own exhaust fumes. Never mind that from now until Doomsday there will not be a single day when huge stretches of motorway are not partitioned off with traffic cones. No, our love affair with the fickle mistress that is the internal combustion engine shows no sign of waning.

It's good to know that the millions spent by the car manufacturers on advertising their sleek new models are not going to waste. Cars are now inextricably linked with power, virility and sex appeal. You don't have to be Desmond Morris to realise what a bright red Ferrari Testarossa represents in the phallocentric imagination of the average male driver. Which, incidentally, begs the question: just what does a Reliant Robin represent? A prostate gland, perhaps.

Since most new models look like they've just popped out of the same jelly mould, the adverts seem to say: 'To hell with boring facts and figures; since all cars look much the same, let's just indulge our most ludicrous fantasies'. Cars in TV adverts negotiate fire, brimstone, whirlwinds and roads that turn into spitting cobras. Most bizarrely of all, they seem to be the only vehicle on that twisty mountain road. The characters in adland seem to live in a parallel universe where driving is an orgasmic pleasure rather than a wearisome chore.

Nowadays the siren voices of the advertisers are tempting us to buy one of those rugged 4x4 off-road jobs. These tough workhorses seem very popular down here in Litterdale, where a lot of motorists subscribe to the scouts' motto: Be Prepared. They're prepared, at a moment's notice, to gear down, leave the overcrowded roads behind, and tackle the roughest and most inhospitable terrain... such as the speed-bumps in Tesco's car-park.

Owners of 4x4 vehicles can look down – quite literally – on other drivers, and enjoy the kudos of owning a vehicle with the aerodynamic qualities of a house-brick. Those intimidating 'bull-bars' on the front aren't merely decorative. Okay, the chances of running into a bull – or being charged by a rampaging rhino – are pretty slim, even in Litterdale. But pedestrians can get aggressive too. Especially if they've just been knocked over by a 4x4 driver who's preoccupied by taking a call on his mobile phone. And a little old lady, once roused to anger, can do a lot of damage to expensive paintwork with a shopping trolley and a bone-handed umbrella.

Ownership isn't enough, of course; 4x4 owners like their possessions to be reassuringly obsequious too. So when they point the key-fob at their car, it flashes its lights and gives an answering 'beep'. 'I am yours, O powerful one', it seems to be saying, 'what might be your bidding?'

Having done their damnedest to make city life well-nigh intolerable, the car manufacturers are making life in the country equally unpleasant. So the ads for these outsize Tonka toys tend to show them perched on a mountain-top, with a spectacular landscape as a mouth-watering backdrop. My usual response is: 'Wonderful landscape; shame there's some 4x4 lunatic parked smack in the middle of it'.

P.T. Barnum knew his stuff. 'No-one ever went broke by over-estimating the public's intelligence,' he once said, with the cynicism of the born salesman. And what these ads seem to be suggesting is that the countryside is just one big adventure playground for people (oh, all right, *men*...) who have plenty of 'poke' under the bonnet... but not a lot upstairs. Combine the body of a grown man, the recreational tastes of a hyperactive six-year-old and the mental agility of a rocking horse... and you have a potent force when behind a wheel. Dressed in their khaki fatigues they can indulge the kind of fantasies that engage tiny minds when national service is but a distant memory.

Every weekend they'll meet up in Litterdale with like-minded loons, with the aim of churning up as much countryside as possible in the course of an eventful afternoon. They'll transform ancient 'green lanes' into boggy morasses, just for the hell of it. They don't feel they've had a proper day out unless they and their tank-like vehicles are covered in mud.

There's a certain novelty value in seeing a 4x4 streaked with mud, instead of being filled with kiddy-seats, green wellies and a week's worth of bagged-up supermarket shopping. It's just a shame that the cherished landscapes around Litterdale have to take the brunt of the off-roaders' warlike fantasies. Perhaps we could convert one of the limestone quarries into a real assault course for these off-road guys, with a few well-hidden land-mines to improve their driving skills and keep their minds on the job. Just a thought...

*

Smack in the middle of Litterdale you will find a pair of handsome pubs. The casual visitor may wonder why a village as small as

Litterdale should warrant two such substantial inns. The truth is that the village hasn't always been the peaceful backwater it appears today. Litterdale lies on what once was the London road, and the stage-coaches stopped here to change horses and take on new passengers.

In those far-off days the roads joined town to town, and village to village, like pearls strung along a necklace. It's different today, of course. We can built straighter roads now (and are busy carving up our beautiful landscapes to accommodate them) but they strenuously avoid towns, villages and anywhere else you might want to go. Archaeologists of the future will unearth the remains of our late-twentieth century road network with a mixture of awe and amazement. They'll look back on their ancestors' titanic efforts in building roads that seem merely to link a series of identical eateries and service stations. Twenty years after the demise of the internal combustion engine we'll see the car for what it's always been: an experiment that didn't work.

These two inns continue to stare at each other across the broad street, and across the centuries. The Swan and the Fox share an architectural style, perhaps even the same builder. Small details – such as the heavy stone lintels and the pillars on either side of the entrance doors – announce that these aren't just run-of-the-mill village pubs. The old stable blocks are reminders of why two such inns were built here in the first place. The differences between these establishments only become apparent once you step inside.

The Swan is aptly named. The staff, and the pub itself, seem to float serenely along through still waters. There's a calm, unruffled air that proves happily contagious. Of course, it takes a lot of hard work behind the scenes to make catering appear so effortless. The staff give the impression that they actually enjoy working here, which is quite a novelty in itself. They're mostly young girls, smartly dressed in white blouses and black skirts. Intriguingly, they all seem to fall short, by the tiniest margin, of being absolutely gorgeous. They're wonderfully efficient and a little bit shy.

In the Fox the scene is very different. It's entertaining – in a grim, voyeuristic kind of way – to watch an ill-assorted team of incompetents and malcontents bring the noble art of catering down to the level of a playground squabble. The moment you walk in, you are assailed by prohibitions. Considering that Litterdale lies smack in the middle of some of the White Peak's finest countryside, you wonder immediately about the mental equilibrium of a landlord who erects a notice stating: 'No Walkers'.

He neatly reverses the traditional relationship between landlord and customer, by regaling those drinkers foolish enough to drink at the bar with a seemingly endless litany of complaints and grievances about the iniquities of the landlord's lot. When things are quiet, 'It's hardly worth opening the doors', and then, on those rare occasions when the pub suddenly fills up with thirsty customers, he'll shake his head wearily and confide that, 'They'll all want serving, you know'. The more disreputable locals quite like it; his tirades match their mood, but the uncommitted drinker soon gets the idea that there are an awful lot of other pubs to go to.

The landlord is a man who should never have ventured into the licensed trade. Someone with his welfare at heart (his anger management therapist or, failing that, his accountant) should have warned him that, 'It's a people business', and suggested a career more in keeping with his meagre talents. Some walk of life in which bluntness and an almost limitless antagonism towards his fellow man were no bar to making a living: an angler's bait shop, perhaps, or a key-cutting franchise.

His wife is the sort of woman for whom the description 'mousy' would seem like unwarranted flattery. Her every word and gesture speak of a life filled with disappointment. She spends most of her time drinking ever more generous slugs of sweet sherry and comparing her spouse (unfavourably, on every conceivable count) with her first husband. To discourage diners, she hides the menus. Whenever she's asked, 'Are you cooking tonight?' her response is bafflingly enigmatic: 'I hadn't planned to'. Most people take the hint and sidle towards the door, though every now and again a customer will be hungry enough to persevere in his quest for a square meal. Even then, the florid descriptions (*poisson, pommes frites avec pois mushy*) cannot disguise the unimaginative fare on offer.

Across the road at the Swan a food order initiates a seamlessly orchestrated series of events, culminating with a rosy-cheeked waitress sliding a hearty plateful under your nose. At the Fox, on the other hand, a food order sets off a series of unconnected events which culminate in blind panic. The kitchen staff give convincing impressions of people who have never prepared a meal before. Using the smoke alarm as a food-timer, they fill the pub with the overpowering smell of stale and over-heated cooking fat.

Every lunchtime seems to end the same way: with sounds of crockery smashing against the wall, screams of recrimination, the slamming of doors, the wail of a fire engine's siren, and the cook – an unshaven man with a grubby vest and singed eyebrows – sitting at the bar cradling a double whisky, trying to stop his hands shaking.

If you want to take your mum somewhere quiet for Sunday lunch, or are looking for a pleasant venue where you can try to mollify a financially rapacious ex-wife... then, of course, the Swan fits the bill admirably. But if, like me, you are blessed with the priceless ability to laugh at other people's misfortunes, and enjoy watching the discomfiture of the chronically inept... then I have to admit that, yes, the Fox is the only place in Litterdale to spend 'Unhappy Hour'.

✳

It's August in Litterdale: high summer, when the air is still and balmy, and the limestone scars gleam whitely beneath skies of unclouded blue. Swallows, swifts and martins race and scream above the village, seemingly for the sheer joy of scything effortlessly through the air. There's no better time of the year to skive, loaf, dawdle, dally, hang loose, take things easy, stand and stare, shoot the breeze, twiddle our thumbs, kick our heels, and generally let the grass grow under our feet. Here in Litterdale we have learned to enjoy the lexicon of leisure.

The warm weather encourages locals and visitors alike to don the skimpiest of outfits compatible with not being arrested for outraging public decency. We get an enticing glimpse of what life in Litterdale might be like if, thanks to global warming, we were blessed with a Mediterranean climate the whole year round… instead of just these dog-days of summer. Young lads loll around on the village green, trying to look as cool as possible despite the obvious ravages of adolescent acne. Young girls take part in an impromptu festival of belly buttons. Even the older folk, not generally given to excess, get in the mood and leave their thermal vests at home.

This would be a good time to put a house up for sale; prospective buyers would take little persuading that Litterdale might be the ideal place to escape from the rat-race or enjoy a tranquil retirement. The country life – spent dead-heading roses, trimming hedges and quaffing schooners of cream sherry – looks an attractive option to jaded wage-slaves.

But appearances can be deceptive. Townies looking to swap the crime and grime of the city for what they fondly imagine will be a rural idyll, are setting themselves up for disappointment. Men who have earned their money in town tend to see the countryside as a recreational amenity. An extension of the gym and the wine bar, where stressed-out executives can unwind by drinking in a gorgeous view (preferably through the windscreen of a stationary Range Rover) and reciting a restorative mantra of FT100 indices. Blissfully unaware that proper farming represents a lifetime of mindless, back-breaking labour, working from dawn to dusk seven days a week (with maybe a couple of days off each year to attend Smithfield Show or a seminar about bulls' semen), they feel the urge to get back to the land.

Men dream of a less-acquisitive lifestyle in the country, unaware that the competitive flame can't be doused so easily. Having spent their formative years stuck in rush-hour traffic, extending the hand (or, at least, the middle digit) of friendship to their fellow drivers, they find that driving in the country is not as much fun as they thought it would be. It's frustrating to crawl for mile after twisty mile in the slippery wake of a slurry-laden tractor, whose driver regards traffic signals of any kind as entirely optional.

Their wives have time on their hands and a rosy view of country life that stems from knowing nothing whatsoever about it. A diet of glossy lifestyle magazines and shampoo adverts has given them unrealistic, soft-focus visions of traipsing around a herb garden in a Laura Ashley frock, with a basket of meadow flowers hung decorously over one arm. They order what the salesman promised was a 'farmhouse kitchen' – all stripped pine and terracotta tiles – not realising that a genuine farmhouse kitchen is more likely to resemble a charnel house or motorbike mechanic's workshop.

In a doomed attempt to ingratiate themselves with the locals, the newcomers take up country pursuits. The men develop an unhealthy interest in killing small defenceless animals – dispatching them with a Purdey shotgun, pack of hounds or a light, last-minute touch on the power steering. The women attend Women's Institute meetings: draughty evenings in village halls entering Most Exciting Tea-towel Competitions.

It doesn't work, of course; after a few months of attempted integration the newcomers will bow to the inevitable. They'll spend more and more of their leisure hours with other disgruntled exiles from the city. Liquor-fuelled evenings when they can let down their defences and admit that the much-vaunted attractions of country life are just lies and innuendo, propagated shamelessly by estate agents and the editors of those lifestyle magazines. Amongst friends they'll mutter conspiratorially about terse, unfriendly farmers, whose eyebrows meet in the middle and who seem to appear – without warning, their clothes in disarray – from sheep-fold and byre.

Once the newcomers have taken off those rose-tinted spectacles, it can be the devil of a job to find them again. Aspects of country life that once seemed quaint and endearing now merely irritate. Instead of filling their lungs with that clean country air, all they can smell is the gut-wrenching, sinus-clearing stench of slurry. They realise, too late, why the Old Rectory had remained empty for so long before they moved in; the apprentice bell-ringers in the church next door spend every Sunday morning trying, in vain, to orchestrate some rudimentary chime.

For the locals, sunning themselves on a hot summer day, the appearance of a removal van is worth a muted cheer. It means that another defeated couple is packing up their goods, chattels and shattered dreams of country living, and heading back to the leafy blandness of suburbia. Another 'For Sale' sign will appear. Another family will be seduced by the prospect of life in Litterdale. Perhaps they'll have no sense of smell. Perhaps they'll be as deaf as the posts that line our village green. For their sakes, we can only hope so.

✸

AUTUMN

Even to consider spending a sunny bank holiday in Litterdale, you would need to love mankind with an unnatural intensity. The village gets so packed with visitors that whatever they've come to see tends to be hidden by the hordes. Those who run the craft-shops, tea-rooms and pubs rub their hands with undisguised glee, of course; they can sniff money in the air. It mingles with the aroma of factor 15 sun-block and whipped ice cream to create a fragrant pot-pourri of profit. Everybody else in the village regards a bank holiday as a good opportunity to visit uncherished relatives in town or apply that second coat of Artex to the back bedroom ceiling.

The Litterdale Show is a late-summer extravaganza that promises something for everybody and a welcome respite from the workaday routine. The event is known – at least by newcomers to Litterdale, accustomed to rather more sophisticated entertainments – as the 'fête worse than death'. To the show committee it's a Family Fun Day, though you have to think twice about any event that includes the words 'Family' and 'Fun' in the same sentence.

A field just outside Litterdale is transformed, for one day each year, into a rural playground filled with marquees, stalls and show-rings. We used to get the local squire to cut the ribbon and declare the show open, but times are hard for the local aristocracy. He still lives in the Big House, but it's mortgaged up to the hilt. The older villagers may doff their caps to him, but his jacket is suspiciously threadbare. And the squire's customary privileges have all but disappeared; even deflowering virgins is something he can't take for granted these days. Opening Litterdale Show was his last public duty, and now that's gone too. This year the committee has made a break with tradition, and invited a second-string soap actress from daytime TV to do the honours instead.

The show provides an opportunity for the local farmers to get together and monopolise the bar in the beer tent. Once they've been let off the leash for the day, they can put a fair few pints away. When they emerge, blinking at the sudden exposure to the mid-afternoon sunshine, they cast covetous eyes over the brand-new tractors and combines on display. They try to convince themselves how their work-rate would increase if they had heated seats, double-glazed windows and a state-of-the-art in-cab CD system. And some gleaming new paintwork instead of the unprepossessing two-tone colour scheme – rust and primer – that typifies the clapped-out tractors languishing back on the farm.

There's always a motor-cycle dare-devil who risks life and limb by jumping over a line of cars. But the stakes are raised every year. It gets harder and harder to impress a jaded audience weaned on the special effects of blockbuster films. Our fearless rider will attempt the usual stunt… but this time he'll be towing a caravan behind him. He's unnervingly confident, though everybody else knows it can only end in tears.

You can find stalls selling all manner of country clothing. With their one indispensible fashion accessory being baling twine, the farmers don't take much heed. But well-heeled newcomers to Litterdale like to reinforce their country credentials and give their gold credit cards a bit of hammer. They'll try on quilted waistcoats that resemble nothing so much as the insulation lagging around an old-fashioned central-heating boiler. And those ubiquitous waxed jackets, from a rather upmarket stall offering 'Mud-coloured Clothing to the

Gentry'. After they've completed the ensemble with a pair of green wellies, they reckon they really look the part.

The vicar's wife runs the children's pet show. When it comes to picking a winner, it would take the wisdom of Solomon to choose between the rival claims of a guinea pig and a shaggy Shetland pony. So, since they're all God's creatures, every pet gets a prize.

I understand her quandary, because I recall doing the same job a few years back. A young lad arrived with an impenetrable stutter and a sturdy cardboard box clutched to his chest. 'So what have you got in there?' I asked him. 'It's a mu, mu, mu, mmmm… ,' he struggled. 'What's that?' I said, 'a mouse?' He shook his head, sadly, and had another painful stab at the elusive M-word. I could see the afternoon drifting away, so I said, 'Let's have a look, then,' and lifted up a flap. Out of the box, with a lot of noise and a flurry of feathers, flew a magpie. It didn't stick around for the judging. The lad gazed after it, his mouth still opening and closing wordlessly like a goldfish. I don't know whether the first prize penant was sufficient compensation for losing his magpie. The other kids didn't seem to mind, and at least it made me feel a bit better.

Litterdale Show is a bittersweet occasion. It's good to wander round and chat with old friends, but we're all aware that the show marks the end of summer. There's a distinct nip in the air as the guy-ropes are loosened and the tent-pegs are pulled out. Already the swallows are gathering excitedly on the telephone wires. Young lads have swapped bats and stumps for a football, and throw their jackets down on the grass for goal-posts.

Litterdale's cricket team has just one game left to play, and Dennis, the team captain, is hoping to finish the season on a high note. He's preparing the wicket on his own. His team-mates have conveniently forgotten to turn up, as usual, but they'll all be there for the match. He ought to be disgruntled… but he's not. When he's walking behind an elderly Acme mower, with the sun on his back and the sweet scent of new-mown grass in the air, the captain of the Litterdale XI is convinced that he has the ropes of life firmly in his grasp. For a few intoxicating moments he is a truly happy man.

Litterdale, as the tourist brochures never tire of telling us, lies smack in the middle of the White Peak, surrounded by rolling hills that seem to invite you to explore them. Nevertheless, there are many visitors to Litterdale who prove remarkably resistant to the siren voices of the countryside. They like the idea that Litterdale is *in* the countryside – that's why they come – but all that greenery is just something to drive through on the way there and on the way home. They feel more comfortable viewing the countryside through the windscreen of what we used to call a family saloon. If they are assailed by any nasty smells, they can just wind the windows up to create a safe, hermetically-sealed environment: Tupperware on wheels.

But autumn brings other visitors, too. A worked-out limestone quarry a couple of miles from Litterdale is quietly going back to nature. Ten years ago it was a site of noise and industry, with the surrounding countryside lent a surreal, almost moonlit appearance by a powdering of rock-dust. But now the quarry is filled with water and the rocky margins are softened by bullrushes and yellow irises; an unprepossessing eyesore is slowly becoming Litterdale's own little Serengheti. The lake has become a magnet, every spring and autumn, for migrating birds. And in their wake come hordes of bird-watchers.

I can thank my dad for fostering my own interest in bird-watching. As a toddler I used to crawl around the garden, and pick up whatever caught my eye. Birds' feathers were probably the least objectionable of these tiny treasures. Still at that blissful age when parents are all-knowing, I'd ask my dad to identify them. Bless him, he didn't just tell me to go away and stop wasting his time. He'd fold up his newspaper and ascribe a different bird's name to every single feather I brought him. No doubt he mugged up with a bird book; how else would a handful of feathers, collected from a small village garden, have included capercaillie, red kite and bearded tit?

His relaxed attitude to ornithological identification helped to sow the seeds of a lifelong hobby that's brought me enormous pleasure over the intervening years, for no greater cost than a field-guide to British birds and a pair of binoculars. A few friends shared my childhood interest, and our gardens became bird reserves in miniature. We'd see how many species we could log in our own locale, and enter the sightings in our nature diaries. But there are only so many species that can be lured to a garden with half a coconut and a handful of bird-seed. And our knowledge of birds was soon outstripped by the need to spot less common species. It got quite competitive, as we tried to beat each other's tally. One day we nearly came to blows about an over-optimistic sighting of a crested tit which, when not eating peanuts on my chum's bird-table, would otherwise only occur in dense conifer forests in the Scottish Highlands.

These childish spats were soon forgotten. It seemed silly to argue about birds, when we should just be enjoying them. In short, we grew up. But little did we know that this ludicrously competitive aspect is actually the *raison d'être* of a barmy army of adult bird watchers, known as 'twitchers'. These are men (the vast majority are men, at least) who would happily sell their grandmothers into the white slave trade if this might add a new bird to their 'life list'. Like ornithological Casanovas, the thrill is in the chase. No sooner have they ticked off a new species than they're off in search of the next conquest.

They share the characteristics of obsessives everywhere. The most extreme of religious fundamentalists would nod in appreciative recognition of their single-mindedness. Some of our twitchers are just too busy to work. Once their life lists of British birds creep towards a figure of 450, it gets pretty hard to add new 'ticks'. So, armed with pagers and mobile phones, they are ready, at the drop of a woolly hat, to respond to the sighting of some rare bird. Any place, any time. Wilson's pharolope in Shetland? Rough-legged buzzard in the Scilly Isles? No problem; they just sling a sleeping bag into the car and hit the road.

These twitchers have allowed their lives to get seriously out of kilter. The urge to compete is so strong that even bird-watching is not immune. And yet, what's to stop anyone from claiming he has seen a bird when he hasn't? He may search unsuccessfully to spot some tiny warbler that all his birding colleagues have seen, but eventually decide to claim the sighting anyway. Who's to know? This is why birders are such a paranoid bunch; they never know whether other twitchers are as mendacious as they are themselves. But it's a reasonable guess…

The simple, unalloyed pleasures of bird-watching are lost on these loons. It's a neat trick to turn a relaxing pastime into just another stressful rat-race. Their affliction is based on a categorical refusal to look at themselves objectively and think: 'Is this really a suitable thing for a sensible, grown-up man to be doing?'

No matter; the lake at Litterdale is a delightful place for sane bird-watchers (yes, like me…) to while away a few tranquil hours. It teems with wildfowl, especially when the autumn migration is at its height. There's no point in rushing around, ticking off new species, when you can lose yourself in such an animated scene. In any case, there are usually a handful of rarities that turn up each year. And when the twitchers come in their wake – with powerful telescopes on tripods, and eyes ablaze with misplaced passion – it's always fun to irritate them by pointing out, with exaggerated excitement, a commonplace coot or moorhen.

For a lot of visitors to Litterdale – raised on the free-market notion that 'you get what you pay for' – the success of a day out can be reckoned by totting up what they've spent. It's a simple calculation. Their pockets are empty by the time they head for home… *ergo*, they must have had a good time.

There's a love-hate relationship between the visitors and the pub landlords of Litterdale. Visitors bring money into the village, and they're not shy of spending it. Our pub landlords rub their hands together – in an obsequious, Basil Fawlty kind of way – whenever a well-heeled family walks into their establishment. A few moments of mental arithmetic – totting up the cost of five bar-meals, two rounds of drinks and a tip – promises a tidy sum. The children's drinks –

tiny bottles of fizzy pop – are the most profitable line of all. The artificial colourings make small children hyperactive, so that harassed parents will buy them another bottle in the mistaken belief that it will quiet them down. It's a real money-spinner.

By this time of the year, though, visitor numbers have dwindled to a mere trickle. Our pub landlords can stop looking so relentlessly cheerful, which is a relief. But pubs still need customers, and that's a worry. So now is the time to win back the custom of the local farmers, plough-jockeys, hired hands, senior citizens and disaffected youth: the very people who were least welcome during the heady summer months. Into winter storage go the patio furniture, the colourful umbrellas and the over-priced menus with their flowery euphemisms. Back come the pool table, the dart board and the man-sized chip butties. The landlords will have to endure the more robust behaviour of this boisterous clientele... but only until next Easter, when the tourist season will begin again.

Bill, our tourism officer, is doing his best to attract visitors 'out of season', when Litterdale presents a less frenetic face to the world. And this year's theme is walking. Seasoned hikers need little persuading about the pleasures of walking the White Peak. They already come in numbers to enjoy the rolling hills and the secluded limestone dales. But, almost by definition, they tend to be a self-reliant bunch. They come prepared for every eventuality, with haversacks full of waterproofs, maps, blister cream, sandwiches and flasks of tea. They don't mooch around Litterdale, throwing their money around; they look to the hills instead. Within ten minutes of arriving in Litterdale, they are just specks disappearing over the first horizon.

If it's tranquillity you want, then it's easily found on the breezy tops. After a stiff climb you can reward yourself with a panoramic view down to Litterdale – wedged into the valley bottom by the folds of the hills.

For every accomplished hiker, however, there are dozens of people whose walking experience extends no further than a brief expedition down to the corner shop to buy a paper and twenty Bensons. People who have never knowingly crossed a contour line. And it's these very people who are currently being wooed by Bill. It's a tactic fraught with pitfalls, as he is beginning to realise.

They come ill-prepared for a change in the weather, or the ravages of hunger and thirst – assuming, unwisely, that there'll be a take-away over the crest of every hill. All they have is a little brochure about the newly inaugurated Litterdale Way: a splendid ramble that incorporates some of the loveliest countryside around the village. The brochure is Bill's proud handiwork; in theory, at least, it offers an easily-followed route.

So much for theory. A few disgruntled farmers have tossed the waymarking signs over the nearest hedge or – more insidiously – rotated the finger-posts through ninety degrees. The result is a lot of disorientated walkers staring uncomprehendingly at their brochures, holding them first one way and then the other. The only thing they are sure of is that they are hopelessly lost.

This is the moment that panic sets in. The hills that looked so pretty through the windscreen of a speeding car now seem gloomily oppressive. The trees creak and bend alarmingly in the stiffening wind. Storm clouds gather. Grouse take off with heart-stopping suddenness, their call a mocking 'Go back, go back'. Circling curlews look more like vultures, sensing that a meal is in the offing.

Groups of terrified walkers are emptying out their pockets. Some, fearing the worst, are scribbling notes to their loved ones. Others are pooling their meagre resources, wondering how long they would survive on a packet of Jaffa Cakes and a can of Irn Bru. And then someone, cutting through the rising hysteria, wonders, 'Would this be any use?' and produces a mobile phone. *Any use*? It's a godsend…

Litterdale's hill rescue service is manned by a dedicated crew of men who would give Chris Bonnington a run for his money in a Chris Bonnington look-alike contest. In the past they've mustered every few weeks to bring injured walkers down from the tops. But now the hills are full of nincompoops with mobile phones, who seem to regard the rescuers as a convenient extension of room service. They have only the vaguest idea of what constitutes an emergency, which is why the rescue service are taking an increasing number of calls requesting they deliver 'a new pair of boot-laces' or 'some milk for the tea, we forgot to bring any'. The callers don't have a clue where they are; 'If we *knew* where we were, we wouldn't be ringing you, would we?'

It's Bill's turn to get a phone-call – from the leader of the hill rescue service. Since he doesn't drink in the Fox – the more disreputable of the village's two pubs – he's not used to hearing this kind of language. When he's able to get a word in edgeways he makes a solemn promise: there'll be no more brochures inviting ill-equipped townies to explore the lovely landscapes around Litterdale.

WINTER

It's December in Litterdale and the villagers mostly have the place to themselves once more. There's a thin layer of ice on the village duckpond, which gives the mallards the appearance of miniature ice-breakers as they make laboured progress across the water. The kids come to feed them with stale bread, and to send stones skittering across the ice. The air is thin and sharp, carrying their shrill, excited voices far beyond the village. No wonder they're excited; they know Christmas is nearly here.

When visitors *do* come in winter, it's usually over Christmas or New Year, and mostly to get away from their loved ones for a few days. It doesn't matter that the December sun has set by mid-afternoon; they don't come to take long hikes over the hills. A brief stroll down to the Swan, wrapped up like sausage rolls against a cold wind, is a more likely scenario. Stone-flagged floors, log fires, a brandy to swirl lazily around a balloon glass; '*This* is more like it', they think, as they settle back into comfortable wing-back chairs.

What the visitors are looking for is a village Christmas, a Breughel painting brought to life. A bare and brittle landscape peopled with tiny figures, all going about their business. And, amazingly, this is pretty much what Litterdale *does* look like in winter. The colour is drained from the landscape, as photosynthesis shuts down operations till spring, reducing the scene to tone, line and texture; the tracery of dry stone walls in the valley, leafless trees silhouetted against a fretful winter sky, sturdy stone houses built to withstand the worst of Pennine weather.

The farmers are out in the fields – come rain, come shine – doing those boring but essential jobs. Even though nothing is growing, the farmers don't think: 'Hmm, things are a bit quiet on the farm. Maybe I'll take a fortnight off, put my feet up and catch up with some reading.' Hill-farming isn't a job, it's a way of life. It's not something you can put to one side for a few days, like a piece of knitting. Cows need milking twice a day, every day. *They* don't know it's Christmas. Hard, unrewarding work is the farmer's currency; if you were to take that away from them, they'd have nothing.

They don't appreciate being told how lucky they are to be 'in touch with the land and the seasons', especially by city folk on holiday. But if you want to see a red-faced farmer incandescent with fury, just suggest that you're thinking about doing a bit of farming too: a little smallholding, a few animals, maybe some rare breeds of sheep. Yes, what gets the farmers of Litterdale really angry is people who just *play* at being farmers.

We are gearing ourselves up for what we laughingly call the festive season. Ah, Christmas, the time of year when we feel our own shortcomings most acutely. When the gap seems to widen, unbridgeably, between what we wanted to be and what we seem to have become. When we are forced to confront the goodness in the world and the badness that's in *us*.

It's a difficult time of year. No wonder we try to make up for these shortcomings by buying expensive presents for family and friends that seem to have more to go with assuaging guilt than the unalloyed joy of giving. We try to be a little better than we usually think we are. But the odds are stacked against us. 'We only do it for the kids,' we suggest, blithely, as we load up the supermarket trolley with surreal quantities of booze.

Christmas seems to have been going on since mid-October, which means that by the time the celebrations actually arrive, we are heartily sick of tinsel, artificial snow and the CDs of Christmas songs that the landlord of the Swan insists on playing from the moment he opens up to the moment he locks the door, with a heartfelt sigh of relief, at closing time. It's a bizarre notion that anyone sane would want to hear, yet again, Roy Wood's probably certifiable request: I Wish it Could be Christmas Every Day.

But no matter how jaundiced you may feel about Christmas (and I bow to no-one in the depth of my distaste for the cynical spending-spree that it has become), it still retains the power to melt the stoniest of hearts. At some point between the last of the mince pies and the Queen's speech, you will be ambushed by the 'true spirit' of Christmas. It happens every year, and it's always a surprise.

One year it was my young daughter looking up at me with her big, brown, trusting eyes. Understanding the need for secrecy at this time of year, she refused to divulge what she had bought for me – merely saying, bless her, that 'It isn't a comb'.

Another year we had friends to stay over the holiday. On Christmas day morning all our carefully nurtured notions of sexual equality suddenly evaporated. The women seemed to feel a primordial pull towards cooking the mountain of food we'd bought. And the blokes felt an equally primordial desire to let them get on with it. Our half-hearted attempts to help (just standing around, getting in the way, saying 'Is there anything we can do?') had the desired effect. 'Why don't you go for a walk?' the women said, in the tone of voice they generally used when speaking to small children.

So three blokes, well wrapped-up, wandered out into the pale winter sunshine. As a local, reckoning to know my way around, I hadn't bothered to take a map so, predictably enough, by the time we'd traipsed over the hills for a couple of hours, we were hopelessly lost. With the weather worsening we decided to knock on the door of a nearby farmhouse, and ask for help. The only sign of life was the smoke billowing from the chimney. But when the door opened we looked into a huge farmhouse kitchen, where the whole family were busy preparing food. It looked and smelt wonderful.

The farmer was happy to point us on the right track back home... but first we had to sample the hot toddy he was making. After a good walk in the cold, this tasted wonderful, too, especially as whisky seemed to be the main ingredient. 'You'll have another,' the farmer said, more than once. We sat round that kitchen table, increasingly full of Christmas spirit, until the candles and the lights on the tree were pleasantly blurred... and then staggered home to our own Christmas meal in Litterdale.

Christmas is over for another year; we've had the giving of the presents and the exchanging of the receipts. It wasn't just the goose getting fat; the orgy of eating and drinking has left Litterdale folk inert and listless, hoping that the hangovers will have subsided by the time the Visa bills roll in. To cap it all, everything we bought in December is being flogged off at half-price during the January sales. It's adding insult to insolvency; since we're feeling corpulent and broke it's hard to know whether to tighten our belts or loosen them.

We fantasise about healthy food, strict diet regimes and proper exercise (not merely walking the dog down to the Fox for a swift pint and a bag or two of pork scratchings). New Year's resolutions are made optimistically but are invariably broken: a process that's generally over and done with in the course of a long weekend. If the road to hell really is paved with good intentions, then over-indulgent Litterdale folk won't be needing an extra sweater in the next life.

Tempers are fraying in every Litterdale household. The children are frazzled and hyperactive from playing too many violent computer games. The women have run through their repertoire of recipes for left-over turkey. Bird tables all around the village are crowned with turkey carcasses – it's like some macabre ceremony – allowing the blue tits and sparrows to pick the bones clean. The men are queasy and disorientated. The holiday drags on, allowing them time to mull over important questions, like: 'Why did I spend so much money just to give myself liver damage?'

Life's familiar tempo has been disrupted over the holiday; some folk don't even know what day it is. Everyone seems relieved at the prospect of getting back to normal. After so much inactivity, the working week has an unaccustomed appeal. Families can survive pretty well on a diet of five days' work and two days of leisure. When those two days stretch into double figures, even the most harmonious families can get crabby and argumentative.

It has been raining for days. A photographer might enjoy the gilded reflections of street-lamps in puddles, and the way that the cobbles glisten in the side-streets of Litterdale. But everybody else just sees cloudy skies, with spring a very distant prospect indeed. The little river that runs through Litterdale has been transformed into a torrent as it surges swollenly beneath the old packhorse bridge. It looks like winter stew on the boil.

There are half a dozen days each year – mostly in winter – when the air is hypnotically clear. When you can stand on top of one of the hills that cradle the village of Litterdale, and see for miles. When you feel you need only to stretch out a hand to be able to touch the furthest horizon. These are special days, magical days, when you're lucky if you're out walking instead of being stuck in the office or workshop. You can't anticipate them.

At this time of the year you may get two dozen dreary days in a row: days when the sun fails to make even a cameo appearance, and the clouds resolutely refuse to lift. The good folk of Litterdale begin to feel gloomy and twitchy from sunlight deprivation. Then, without warning, we wake up one morning to find that the world has been washed clean in the night. Instead of lowering clouds in standard-issue battleship grey, the sky is a rich, regal and unclouded blue. Those same photographers sniff the air, dust down their cameras, and murmur: 'The light, the light…'

The air is clear and still and seems to resonate with the slightest sound. Metal studs on a pair of working boots produce bright, ringing sounds against the cobbles – like a blacksmith overheard striking his anvil in the next village. The noise of a tractor starting up is so familiar around Litterdale that we hardly notice it any more. But on a morning like this we register every judder of a determinedly unmaintained engine; the squeal of an unoiled hinge – and an involuntary oath – as the cab door shuts on cold, careless fingers; the rasping sound of a farmer clearing his throat and depositing a ball of phlegm onto the frosty grass.

Ragged-winged rooks congregate noisily in wind-tossed trees. They can always find something to bicker about. Few sounds exemplify the bare, raw winter landscape like the rooks' cantankerous croaking. Flocks of twittering winter finches scavange for meagre pickings in the field margins: a loose affiliation of chaffinches, greenfinches, goldfinches and bramblings. It's only in such cold weather that they set aside their differences and band together for survival. A wren calls from the thorny heart of a hawthorn hedge. Fieldfares soar across fields dusted with hoar-frost, far from their Arctic breeding grounds.

Pheasants line up on the verges of the quieter roads. Most birds make themselves scarce whenever a car passes, but pheasants can't be bothered. They have a stoical disposition that stems, no doubt, from being shot at by well-heeled businessmen. Stoical and despondent; it's hard for pheasants to look on the bright side when they know what fate has in store. The gamekeeper puts food out for them – there's no need to forage – and the pheasants keep eating. There's nothing much else to do, except to get fatter and fatter. If the gamekeeper were to put out roasting dishes they'd probably just climb in, baste themselves and set the oven to regulo five.

So is it any wonder that some of the pheasants feel suicidal? They stand by the side of the road, thinking: 'Shall I? Shan't I?' and then, on a car's approach, they give a world-weary sigh. Their last thought is: 'Sod it…' as they scuttle beneath the wheels.

There's not a lot happening in Litterdale. We're in that briefest of interludes between the end of the January sales and the appearance – in those same shops, a few weeks later – of the Easter Bunny. The village is almost empty. Maybe it's a flag-day. Maybe the neutron bomb's gone off. Maybe it's just half-day closing.

The landscapes depicted on the now-discarded Christmas cards differ from reality in one startling respect: there's snow on the cards, but none in Litterdale. The truth is, of course, that we are more likely to get white *Easters* than white Christmases. And, on the whole, we're pretty stoical about our weather; if we'd demanded to enjoy a Mediterranean-type climate, soaking up the sun amongst the orange groves, then we'd have thought twice about Derbyshire in the first place. It's not that we're particularly enamoured with snow, either, but we'd still be mildly relieved to see some. A proper snowfall, blanketing the landscape, not just wind-blown flurries that come and go in a matter of minutes.

A winter without snow seems contrary to nature. An unrehearsed departure from a familiar script. An unwelcome reminder that there are forces at work over which we have too little control. We listen to the news, and nod sagely as the planet reels from hurricanes, floods and earthquakes. We're aware of what's going on. No snow: global warming. Dry weather: global warming. Wet weather: global warming. Alternating wet and dry weather: global warming. Protracted periods of especially wet... or dry... or changeable weather: yes, that'll be global warming.

The rain and wind lash relentlessly against our homes in Litterdale – lifting roof slates, permeating badly-pointed façades and driving through cracks in rotten window frames. Like the probing jabs of a quick-handed boxer, the rain seeks out the weak spots in our defences. It mocks the half-baked attempts of artless bodgers to make running repairs to their dilapidated homes. Slapdash DIY that seems overly reliant on cardboard, sticky tape and string, with scrunched-up newspaper to staunch the gaps where the wind whistles straight through.

These houses may have been built to withstand the worst of Pennine weather, but it takes only a few years of wilful neglect to make the local odd-job man shake his head, suck his teeth and retrieve a pencil from behind his ear. A few figures scribbled on the back of a cigarette packet are enough to convince cash-strapped villagers that essential repairs will have to be postponed for yet another year.

Bob, Litterdale's postman, is one householder who is tossing and turning through many a sleepless winter night, listening for the tell-tales signs that foretell disaster: the creaking of floorboards, the insistent 'drip, drip, drip' of water from unlagged pipes and the last, asthmatic gasps from a geriatric central heating boiler. In those wee, small hours a man with an overactive imagination can almost hear the conspiratorial conversations of death-watch beetles, as they draw lots to see which vital, load-bearing stanchion they'll chomp through next.

No sooner has Bob fallen into a troubled, fitful sleep than the ringing of the alarm clock makes him sit bolt upright, like a mummy in one of those old black and white horror films. The bell is louder than most folk might choose, but a postman needs something insistent to oust him from a warm bed at five o'clock in the morning. Cath rolls over, with a couple more hours of sleep in mind, taking most of the duvet with her.

It's at times like this that Bob wishes he could number more plumbers and electricians among his acquaintances, and fewer traditional folk singers. Michael Schumacher would feel very much at home in Bob and Cath's house: it's the pits. There are so many jobs that need doing – both inside the house and out – that the prospect overwhelms him. He can't decide where to start, no matter how many hints Cath drops, so he never makes a start at all.

He looks on with a mixture of envy and self-reproach as his neighbours make running repairs to their homes. Bob, too, longs for snow; planting the first footprints of the morning in a fresh snowfall, as he makes his rounds. Snow is so egalitarian. For a few blissful days it makes his unkempt, weed-strewn garden look as good as everyone else's.

It's Sunday morning, so Bob indulges in one of his favourites ploys to counter Household Neglect Frustration: transforming an untidy heap of branches into a neat pile of split logs and a few baskets of kindling. If the boiler's about to blow, best make contingency plans. It's a simple, repetitive, strangely absorbing task, the perfect antidote to life's more baffling complexities. Passers-by don't ask: 'What the hell are you doing *that* for, Bob?' They instinctively understand a man's primeval need to bludgeon inanimate objects into submission. It's self-explanatory. Bob doesn't need an instruction manual, or a telephone help-line, or an over-paid consultant to tell him what to do. He only needs to bend his back to get warmed twice over: first from the chopping, later from the fire.

He weighs the axe in his hands, finding it reassuringly heavy, and runs a cautious thumb along the blade. He spits on his palms (he doesn't know why, it's just part of the ritual), takes a swing and brings the axe down in a wide arc onto a fat log. 'Thwack', his bank manager's balding head is almost severed from his shoulders. 'Thwack', it rolls along the cobblestones and comes to rest in the gutter. With every frenzied blow, Bob runs through a rosta of retribution; with every week that goes by, the list seems to get longer. By the time he gets around to the bloke who short-changed him down at the newsagent, he's gasping for breath, his brow is glistening with sweat and a morning's work is done.

SPRING

Civic pride is one of those virtues – like politeness and sportsmanship – that we now seem to have abandoned as quaint and old-fashioned. But Norman has an old-fashioned view of things, and he doesn't mind who knows it. With his collarless shirts, waistcoats and mutton-chop whiskers, he even looks like he belongs to another age. Some people may find his behaviour a little baffling but, if pressed on the matter, will offer grudging admiration. To the rest of us he's a saint. Saint Norman of Litterdale.

Norman is a fixer, a handyman, a jack-of-all-trades… and master of quite a few. His neat little house confirms the wisdom of doing those vital jobs a few weeks before they really need to be done. Unlike Bob the postman he doesn't lie awake at night, wondering whether his house will still be standing in the morning. He sleeps the untroubled sleep of a man who is up to speed with his maintenance programme. When a job needs doing, Norman doesn't talk about it… he just does it.

Having given his lawn one last cut, back in autumn, Norman sharpened the blades on his mower, oiled every moving part and covered the machine with a tarpaulin. Now, with spring finally within sight, it only needs a smooth pull on the starter cord to bring his mower purring back to life. While Norman is traversing a front lawn that a Wimbledon groundsman would be proud of, everybody else in Litterdale is dragging rusty mowers out of garden sheds and trying, in vain, to breath life into seized-up engines.

They and their lawn-mowers eventually find their way to Norman's workshop. He lets them down easy. Instead of giving them a lecture of mild reproof (on the theme of 'spoiling the ship for a ha'porth of tar') he'll get their machines purring too. He'll take a fiver in payment, a fraction of what an overhaul would cost in town. He knows it salves his neighbours' consciences. And they may have to wait a few days, since everyone brings him their mowers at exactly the same time. Norman is never tempted to remind his more feckless neighbours just how feckless they are. Or if he does feel the temptation, he never gives into it. He should be smug, but he's not. If he had a halo it would be buffed and polished till it gleamed, but he wouldn't dream of wearing it in public.

Litterdale belongs to Norman. Most people are fiercely proprietorial about their little fiefdoms. When they trim a hedge, they go to the limit of their property... and not an inch further. It just wouldn't occur to them to pop next door and say: 'I'm tidying up my bit of the hedge, shall I do yours while I've got the clippers out?' The result looks ludicrous, of course. But Norman has a stake in the village that has nothing to do with deeds, contracts and boundary walls. When he says: 'It's my village', he isn't merely confirming that he was born here fifty-three years ago and that, with luck, he'll be buried here too. It's his village because he looks after it.

We live in a litigious age when, instead of taking responsibility for ourselves when accidents happen, we immediately look for someone else to blame. If a careless pedestrian trips over a flag-stone and turns an ankle, his first response, as likely as not, will be to sue the council. It's 'their' responsibility. 'They' should do something about it. But the wheels of local bureaucracy are notoriously slow in turning. By the time a council workman turns up, rips up the offending flag-stone and makes an ugly repair with a barrow-load of lumpy pitch, half a dozen more Litterdale folk may be nursing swollen ankles.

Norman takes a pride in his little fiefdom too, and chases any cat away that might even be thinking of 'depositing' on his beautifully manicured front lawn. But his gaze extends far beyond his own garden wall; whenever he spies some little corner of Litterdale that needs sprucing up, he takes action. Instead of dashing off a stroppy letter to the council, he changes into his overalls and sets off with his canvas bag of tools to put matters right. Thanks to Norman's efforts, the flag-stones fit together as snugly as pieces in a jigsaw. The war memorial is free from the droppings of unpatriotic pigeons: not just for Poppy Day, but all year round. We can thank the council for putting up hanging baskets of flowers each year, but it's Norman who actually remembers to water them. The sign that welcomes careful drivers to Litterdale can always be read by day-trippers, because Norman gives it a wipe with a damp cloth every time he passes.

Litterdale is a regular prize-winner in the Best Kept Village Competition. When the time comes for the awards to be handed out, the local councillors are happy to accept the judges' plaudits. The mayor and his cronies ('The chain gang', as Norman calls them, dismissively) need no second bidding to crawl out of the woodwork whenever there's an opportunity to claim credit for someone else's work. They always have a banal soundbite at the ready, and smile their ferocious smiles for the photographer of the *Litterdale Times*. For those who give their time to local politics – freely and without thought of personal gain – these occasions act like an intravenous shot of testosterone.

It's Norman who should be up there on the podium, instead of standing in the crowd and applauding these self-important phonies. But he doesn't mind, and he's not bitter about being passed over, thoughtlessly, when the vote of thanks is given. He's seen councillors come and go over the years and, candidly, he wouldn't give a bucket of warm spit for the lot of them. Norman has a different agenda altogether. He's a free spirit, an independent thinker... almost – whisper it – an anarchist. He won't be standing for office, when the local elections come around again, but he'll be ready this spring with his sharpening stone and oil-can when the first knackered lawn-mower arrives in his workshop.

It's Spring in Litterdale, so a young man's fancy turns, naturally enough, to landscape photography. Well, that's Frank's fancy anyway. His working week is spent juggling figures. He'd taken his old math's teacher's advice to heart, believing that there is, indeed, safety in numbers. It's not a bad job, the money's okay and there's no heavy lifting. But even though accountancy pays the bills, his heart's not really in it. By the middle of each week, the figures are starting to crawl over the pages of his ledgers like foraging ants. By the time Friday rolls around, he's getting cabin fever.

Every few minutes his attention is distracted by the view from the window of his airless office. It's 'four seasons in one day' weather outside, the sort of weather that makes a photographer's shutter finger twitch, like a trigger-happy gunman in a bar full of strangers. One minute the storm clouds gather menacingly, and somebody around Litterdale is getting severely rained on. The next minute the clouds part, magically, and a slim pencil of light sweeps across the landscape, like a prison searchlight in an old James Cagney movie, searching for a farmhouse, or a hilltop or a ribbon of road to illuminate against the gloom. Frank holds a biro up to his cheek and clicks it at the decisive moment that the composition comes together. He can't help it, it's just force of habit.

There's no doubt about it, Frank would rather be a landscape photographer than an accountant. But he has to keep it as a hobby, a weekend passion, and maybe that's for the best. Most people in Litterdale have at least one of his framed photographs displayed on the wall. At Christmas time his friends and relatives have learned to feign appreciative surprise when they are presented with yet another moody landscape print. They've learned that: 'It's beautiful, Frank' is all that's required by way of response, not: 'If you'd just moved a few yards to the left, Frank, you wouldn't have had that telegraph pole in the picture…'

Bob the postman has one of Frank's pictures hanging in his living room. It hides one of the damp patches that have appeared, due to Bob's apparent inability to replace the roof-tiles that were blown away in the winter winds. Bob and Cath finally got married last year.

Not before time, it was said, since they've been living together for years. They've got kids too.

Bob was looking, as usual, to save money. What had seemed like a good idea, when he proposed to Cath, after a few drinks in the Swan, was soon getting out of hand. Bob's wedding suggestion – a perfunctory union down at the Registry Office, followed by a pie and pea supper in the Fox – seemed distinctly at odds with Cath's idea of what a wedding should be. A church ceremony, white dress, garlands of lilies, bridesmaids, a five-tier cake, a reception in a marquee, a sit-down meal, champagne – the works.

Bob tried to compromise, even going so far as to suggest a Seventies disco or a karaoke to follow the pie and pea supper. But a mere man of letters is no match against the combined force of a persistent bride-to-be and her family. One by one his defences fell under the onslaught, and everyone in Litterdale agreed that Bob and Cath's was the wedding of the year. One of the few money-saving ideas that *did* survive the rather one-sided wedding negotiations was the choice of photographer. Encouraged by Frank's interest in photography (and discouraged, in equal measure, by the cost of engaging a professional), Bob asked Frank if he would do the honours. Frank, flattered to be asked, but not thinking too clearly, agreed.

Alarm bells should have rung the moment that Frank set up his camera outside the little church in Litterdale. As affable as he is, Frank is not really a 'people person', and the sight of so many wedding guests, dressed up to the nines, got him flustered. A good wedding photographer should combine the tact of a diplomat with the intransigence of a totalitarian dictator. People need to be told – politely – what to do. Forgetting everything he had read in an all-too-brief perusal of the *A–Z of Wedding Photography*, Frank reverted to what he knew best. He thought the scene might be improved with a few of the coloured filters he always kept in his bag.

Big mistake. Instead of being a warm reminder of happy times, Bob and Cath's wedding album is a perennial reminder of what happens when you hire a landscape photographer to chronicle the best day of your life. The sky in each shot is an other-wordly orange… or magenta… or yellow: any colour except the standard-issue Litterdale grey that we know so well. To look at the pictures you'd guess that a nuclear bomb had exploded on the day of the wedding. Instead of being shown off, proudly, to everyone who calls at the house, the wedding album gathers dust on top of the wardrobe.

Bob and Cath have forgiven Frank (well, Bob has, anyway), though Frank still has nightmares about being chased down a long road by a gang of men in top hats and tuxedos. Now he sticks to what he knows best, getting out and about with his trusty Leica, watching the swathes of light as they drift sensuously over the lovely Litterdale landscape. It's his delight to be out at dawn, when the light is doing wondrous things. The local farmers – and maybe Bob on his rounds – are the only ones who see him tramp along the green lanes and out into open country, with his camera bag and his tripod.

The farmers think he's mad; they only get up at dawn because they have to. Frank, in contrast, does it from choice. On those still mornings when the world looks clean and bright and new, the sheer exhilaration of being out in the countryside far outweighs the hassle of those early starts. Big, bland, blue skies fail to set his pulses racing. What Frank enjoys is extremes of weather; his preferred forecast is 'changeable'. The best pictures seem to come at the meeting of weather systems: just before rain and just after. So Frank doesn't feel he's had a proper day's photography unless he's been soaked to the bone at least twice. Whenever he's sheltering from a sudden squall, or sitting on a rock, waiting for the light to do something 'interesting', Frank feels strangely at peace with the world.

Everyday life in our valley is chronicled in the pages of the *Litterdale Times*, a somnolent publication for which even mediocrity would represent an unfeasible ambition. The editor has developed the unerring knack of elevating the dull and the uneventful into headline stories, and burying anything of genuine significance towards the bottom of page five, next to the small ads. On how many other newspapers, for example, would a story be summarily spiked for being 'too interesting'?

The truth, however, is that there's not much call around here for titillating tit-bits, or raunchy headlines. After all, the people the editor writes about every week are the very same people who read the paper. A no-holds-barred exposé of nefarious goings-on might briefly attract a few new readers. But what's the point, the editor reasons, of upsetting people just to double the sales figures? In any case, if his readers were ever to develop an unhealthy interest in salacious stories, they'd be unlikely to salivate over the paper's more mundane headlines, such as this week's offering: Litterdale Man Dies of Natural Causes.

It's easy to knock a local newspaper for being parochial and dull, but it's part of our lives. I read every issue from cover to cover, and those five or six minutes are the highpoint of my week. A subscription to the *Litterdale Times* makes an ideal present for an uncherished relative, or anyone who has left the area and might want to keep abreast of local affairs. There'll be nothing in the paper to disturb delicate sensibilities and, indeed, nothing to make the recipients regret for an instant their decision to have left Litterdale.

The editor – known as 'Scoop' to one and all – sits in his tiny office, stabbing one-fingered at the keys of his ancient Remington typewriter like a demented woodpecker. Provincial journalism courses through his veins; even his conversation can be measured in column inches. So dedicated is he to his chosen craft that not even a breaking story has ever tempted him outdoors. Scoop slept through the moon landings, dozed fitfully as the Berlin Wall came crashing down, and was taking a well-deserved afternoon nap while bombs rained down on Baghdad.

Most of the paper's regular features are concocted by Scoop himself, though an imaginative selection of by-lines gives the illusion of variety. When he's writing the 'Your Stars' column, he's 'Madder Rose', Litterdale's resident seer and sage. The forecasts consist of bland reassurances and undemanding prophesies: 'You'll be getting an important letter this week'. Nothing to give his readers cause for concern. He's particularly kind to Cancerians, on the basis that it can't be much fun to have a star sign named after a disease.

Each week's editorial homily is handled by Scoop in the urbane, authoritative and even-handed guise of 'William Stroll'. He looks at both sides of the issues that concern the good folk of Litterdale, before coming down firmly on the fence. 'Carmine Lake', Litterdale's lady novelist, reviews new books, giving particular prominence to those of local interest. This is the column that gives Scoop most trouble; once he's met his weekly deadline, the prospect of settling down with a book is a less than enthralling prospect.

Financial news comes from 'Barry Wedge', including the day's mickle/muckle exchange rate and the muck/brass proximity quotient. Reports from the livestock auction are kept as brief as possible. With prices being so bad, there seems little point in making our farmers even gloomier than they are already.

Plain-speaking 'Gary Mullet' talks football, chronicling the peregrinations of our local teams as they end this season (like every other season) thrashing about in the relegation zone of the lower leagues. 'Vendetta Lamour' addresses the more intimate problems of troubled readers. Couples whose libidos seem to have gone into hiding without leaving a forwarding address. Bizarrely, not all the letters are made up by Scoop. Our vicar insists on writing his own weekly musings, otherwise Scoop would probably do that too.

There is always a selection of old photographs in each issue, showing how the village looked when the hay was gathered in by hand and the sight of a motor car trundling by was enough to make Litterdale folk rush outside to see what all the fuss was about. People stand around in these old pictures, gazing impassively at the photographer. They give the distinct impression that they have nothing more important to do. Very much like the Litterdale of today, in fact.

The *Litterdale Times* is celebrating its centenary this year. Launched during the last years of Queen Victoria's reign, the paper first found success as a cure for insomnia. Since then, of course, it has witnessed – and largely ignored – the most momentous events of the twentieth century. Scoop had planned to bring out a special facsimile edition of that very first issue, but abandoned the idea when he realised it looked much the same as what he's publishing today. Even that very first headline had a familiar ring to it: Mafeking Relieved, No Litterdale Residents Involved.

A problem shared… is a ready source of gratuitous gossip, and most of the news that's unfit to print in our local paper is readily disseminated over the garden fence, or over a pint in the pub. We don't buy the *Litterdale Times* to be better informed. We buy it because we live here; it's what Litterdale people do. And we'll carry on buying it as long as Scoop's ample figure continues to fill that editorial chair.

SUMMER

Litterdale is a delightful place to live; there's no doubt about it. It's a delightful place to visit, too, which is why a sunny weekend or Bank Holiday finds the village chock-full of people. Once they've arrived, however, they tend to forget whatever it was they came to see, and settle, instead, for mooching around the gift-shops and tea-rooms until their feet start to ache or their car-park tickets expire.

Our village lies smack in the middle of the Peak District National Park: the first landscape to be so designated, half a century ago. Of course, the wage-slaves of our industrial Northern cities had already been escaping, for generations, to these hills and valleys. They had fresh air to breathe – instead of the stale, choking, dusty atmosphere of the mills. Having endured the cacophony of steam-hammers and weaving looms during the working week, they could indeed become 'free men on Sunday'.

It's a truism, of course, that you can't please all the people, all of the time, and the National Park Authority has its critics. There are farmers in Litterdale, for example, who'll prop up the bar at the Fox and complain, to anyone foolish enough to listen, about how hard it is to scrape a living these days. One man's 'treasured landscape' is, after all, another man's workplace. The planning criteria that deter householders from pebble-dashing their cottages, can also frustrate the farmers' attempts to modernise their farms. Farming is a tough way of life at the best of times... and these, most certainly, are not the best of times. When so many farmers' livelihoods are on the line, even the most well-meaning edict from the National Park can seem like red-tape and petty officialdom.

After a couple of beers, the farmers can get pretty agitated. They can foresee a future when they'll be paid not to farm at all, but merely to hang around, leaning on gates, looking suitably rural and picturesque. Misdirecting lost motorists is fine as a harmless pastime, but it's hardly a career move. The farmers keep being told to diversify. But the thought of running some rural theme park, keeping lambs for the kids to pet, makes the farmers shudder. If that's what the future holds, then they might just as well pack it all in now, sell the farm and spend their declining years sunning themselves on a beach in the Bahamas. But they won't, of course. Farming isn't one of those jobs you do until something better turns up; it's for keeps.

Not only is business bad, but even their standing in the community is volatile. One minute the farmers are unsung heroes, stalwart custodians of the countryside. The next minute they're painted as the villains; swanning around in Range Rovers, grubbing up hedgerows, harassing ramblers, spraying crops with noxious pesticides and banking fat subsidy cheques. Old certainties are crumbling. Where farmers once knew their place in the scheme of things, now they're prey to the vicissitudes of bureaucrats in Brussels. No wonder the farmers of Litterdale are disorientated.

It's not just the farmers who complain about living in a National Park. The landlord of the Fox is never really happy unless he's having a good moan. It pains him that he's not allowed to shoot visitors during what is a depressingly long close season. To hear him talk, you'd imagine that visitors come to Litterdale just to make him miserable. On the one hand he loathes visitors; on the other hand he relies on them for much of his income. In an attempt to reconcile these contradictions, he's unfailingly rude to everyone.

This attitude to visitors (can't live with them... can't live without them) is a perennial feature of life in Litterdale. Now, at the height of summer, when the village is heaving with day-trippers, we yearn for tranquil winter days. Yet every winter, when the village isn't tranquil so much as dead, we miss the sounds of summer – especially the reassuring jingle of the cash-tills. If we had a slogan for visitors, it would be: 'Come to lovely Litterdale... but don't stay too long'.

Whenever we start moaning about the influx of visitors, or become complaisant about the lush countryside on our doorsteps, it's a salutary experience to drive to any of the towns and cities that lie beyond the border of the National Park. Sometimes we need to remind ourselves what can happen when green fields are regarded as nothing more than empty building plots.

There was a time when people used to shop in town. Now they drive twenty miles out to some gaudy shopping mall, conveniently sited in the middle of nowhere. Acre after acre of countryside is being sacrificed to our apparently insatiable appetite for retail therapy. And with such breathtaking speed; once we've bulldozed the landscape into submission, the buildings spring up like a virulent rash. Huge, ugly, cavernous warehouses with all the style and cachet of a biscuit tin, surrounded by a car-park the size of Rutland. We're dazzled by the lights of the marketing juggernaut; by the time we come to our senses there may be nothing left but concrete.

Our motorways bludgeon their way through the landscape like a horde of driver ants, consuming everything in their path. Just so that lorries full of corn-flakes can drive up one carriageway, while other lorries, also full of corn-flakes, can hurtle down the other carriageway. We're mortgaging our countryside just to trim a few minutes off our journey times. It's madness.

It's always a relief to see the millstone by the road that tells us we are back in the Peak. Despite the hassles, despite the planning restrictions, despite the endless stream of visitors... it gladdens the heart to be part of a living landscape. So let's give grateful thanks, and a tip of the cap, to the handful of visionary pioneers who fought long and hard to create our National Parks, before our precious landscapes were lost for ever.

✳

We don't have a big problem with crime in Litterdale. It's not some featureless suburb, where people avoid their neighbours. It's a small Peakland village, where everybody knows just about everybody else. Residents can either offer grateful thanks that they live in such a close-knit community, or complain of being surrounded by gossips and eaves-droppers. One thing's for sure, it's hard to keep a secret in Litterdale.

On those blessedly rare occasions when we *do* have a robbery, it's likely to end with a red-faced burglar returning a bin-bag of valuables with an embarrassed shrug of the shoulders and the offer of a conciliatory pint. We have our fair share of roughnecks, of course, but they mostly drink out of harm's way, at the Fox, where the people most at risk from their lager-fuelled outbursts are each other.

To talk of a 'criminal fraternity' makes it all sound rather cosy: a friendly freemasonry of light-fingered gentlemen, with members' ties and special handshakes. But the regulars at the Fox have no need of funny handshakes; an arm twisted sharply up the back is all that's needed to engage the attention of a fellow drinker for a few eye-watering moments.

Whenever there's a shortage of genuine stories to print, the editor of the *Litterdale Times* compensates by composing an eye-catching headline. 'Crime Wave in Litterdale' is a favourite standby. It may tempt a few more people to buy a copy of the paper, though what constitutes a crime wave in Scoop's overheated imagination might, in a more urban setting, be called a quiet weekend. Most Litterdale residents are studiously law-abiding; wearing a loud tie in a built-up area is about the closest they get to a major felony. They're known as careful drivers too – especially those whose tax-discs have expired.

Scoop, however, can draw on years of experience in provincial journalism, and he knows how to make a lot out of little. In a recent editorial he highlighted a litany of crimes that are threatening to rend asunder the fragile fabric of life in rural Derbyshire. Smuggling contraband sheep-dip, rustling geese, forging tickets for the mobile library, and that's just for starters. Even in a community as law-abiding as Litterdale, crime prevention is a mainstay of local politics. Our local councillors read the *Litterdale Times* too, mainly to see if they are in it. Scoop's hard-hitting exposé made them sit up, take notice and recognise a heaven-sent opportunity to bang their own drum even more loudly than usual. They are not the kind of people who hide their light under a bushel. It would be hard to find a bushel large enough.

The council chamber echoes with impassioned debate. The rattling of sabres in a confined space can make quite a din. If a little knowledge is a dangerous thing, then our elected councillors are a lethal proposition. There is one issue, at least, about which they can all agree, on a pleasantly warm summer day. The motion is carried on an enthusiastic show of hands, and a small sum is requisitioned from the Swanning Around on Official Business budget. The rest of us may wonder why our local councillors would even *want* to wear epaulets. No matter. For a few precious minutes there is concord in the chamber (one size fits all, thankfully), but only until a more contentious item comes to the top of the agenda.

As usual, our latest crime wave is largely a product of Scoop's journalistic hyperbole. The miscreant on this occasion is one of Litterdale's senior citizens. He's been forced into a life of petty crime to fund his spiralling snuff habit. Having to find £1.25 a week, *every* week, has made this old codger susceptible to the siren voices of lawlessness. He was caught, red-handed, demanding money with menaces from a Women's Institute Bring and Buy Sale. 'Come on, punk, make my jam,' he'd snarled, unwisely attempting to go cold turkey after a long-term dependence on Old Mill Number 1. It was totally out of character, an aberration. And, once he'd been sedated with a mug of Horlicks, he made a solemn promise to go straight. Straight back to the old folks' home, in fact. If this is what a crime-wave looks like, then Litterdale's more solid citizens ought to be sleeping soundly in their beds at night.

However, once the councillors have got their teeth into a new idea, they're not easily diverted. Which is why the subject of close-circuit TV cameras is currently engaging the hearts and minds of our elected representatives. It sounds an appealing idea... at first. Install a few strategically-sited cameras, and no drinker leaving the Fox after hours would ever again confuse the doorway of the Post Office for a public convenience. Not without starring in his own home movie anyway. Courting couples would think twice before canoodling shamelessly in the bus shelter. We might even discover the identity of the sneak-thief who's been purloining underwear from unattended washing lines these past few months.

The other point of view is equally plausible, and not everyone is happy to have their every move monitored by Big Brother. Security cameras would arguably create as many problems as they'd solve. If it's to be any use at all, camera evidence has to be continually monitored. Who will be prepared to watch hour after hour of unremarkable video-tape, on the off-chance of catching a burglar eyeing up a window of opportunity? Even the most enthusiastic voyeur would soon get bored. Maybe we could market the footage, in 24-hour chunks, as lost classics from the Andy Warhol school of film-making.

Hoarse from haranguing one another, and eager to get home and find a full-length mirror, our councillors end up fudging the issue. They've gone, predictably, for the placebo option. Litterdale will have fake cameras, constructed from shoe-boxes and toilet rolls, mounted in prominent positions around the village. The cost of materials will be minimal, sticky-back plastic mostly. We live in hope that a battery of counterfeit cameras will deter wrong-doers, especially short-sighted ones.

✸

In the Derbyshire police force, a posting to Litterdale is seen as a step down the career ladder. A punishment for past misdeeds, perhaps, or a tranquil semi-retirement for traumatised coppers who can no longer hack it in the city. In crime-fighting terms, Litterdale is a black hole into which a policeman's ambitions can quickly vanish. No serving police officer has ever volunteered for the Litterdale patch; well, not until Sam.

Five years ago Sam Bickerdyke was just another copper on the beat. Pounding the city streets. Upholding the law. Filling his little black book with registration numbers of stolen cars. Writing notes in that strange, stilted language that policemen everywhere feel obliged to use. He tried to learn the off-duty jargon too, the canteen culture that everyone seemed to be talking about. Sam found the canteen easily enough, but precious little culture. Sam is a nature lover, you see. And a bit of a poet.

A more astute recruitment officer might have realised that Sam was temperamentally unsuited for police work. But Sam's father had been a policeman, and his grandfather, and his great-grandfather too. A stern, unsmiling portrait of a man in uniform had been a constant reminder, throughout Sam's childhood, that policing would be his lot. And, to judge from the expression on the bewhiskered face in that sepia-toned photograph, not a particularly happy one. It would have taken more courage than Sam could muster to be the one to break the link in that dynastic chain. No-one ever asked him what he wanted to be when he grew up. Policing wasn't one of many options presented to him. It was the only one.

It seemed, at first, that Sam might have some of the required attributes to be a good policeman. He was tall. He was perceived (wrongly, as it turned out) to be none too bright. He did as he was told. And, conscious of the weight of family expectations, he always tried his best. Predictably, his best was never good enough. Sam found it hard to walk in his father's footsteps. And in his father's boots too; they were at least one size too big for him. Comparisons are odious, of course, but it became painfully obvious to his superiors that Sam wasn't half the policeman his father had been.

His dad was, in fact, the only person who saw a viable future for Sam; he imagined a speedy promotion to the Serious Crime Squad. The rest of the force, unequipped with rose-coloured spectacles, were thinking more in terms of the *Humorous* Crime Squad. Sam, bless him, actually thought a police informant was someone who would give him a tip for the 2.30 at Kempton. Many a discussion began with the vexed question: 'What shall we do with the lad?' So it was a relief all round when Sam decided to jump before he was pushed. The Litterdale posting came up, Sam applied and, in the absence of any other candidates, got the job.

It was a good move. By remaining in the police force, Sam was doing nothing to disgrace the good name of the Bickerdyke family. And by choosing out-of-the-way Litterdale, he ensured that his shortcomings as a police officer would go more or less unnoticed. He has the police house that overlooks the village green. There's a compact police hatchback in the drive. Five years on, it still looks brand new; Sam doesn't do a lot of mileage. It's got a little flashing light, and a siren, but he would feel too embarrassed to use them.

In the front garden is a notice board warning Litterdale locals about the hazards of Colorado Beetles, the wisdom of checking the credentials of unannounced callers and the need for protective clothing when dipping sheep. It's all good advice, especially about the sheep-dip. Having spent too much time dunking sheep in noxious chemicals, some of our local farmers suffer from migraines and sudden lapses of memory (especially around the time when they should be filling in their tax returns).

There's a bird-table in the garden too, which hints at Sam's most abiding interests. He can still hardly believe that he's getting paid to wander round the village, keeping an eye on things. It's not like work at all. His trouser pockets are full of acorns and conkers. Inside his jacket is a well-thumbed field-guide to mosses and liverworts. In the leather pouch where his walkie-talkie ought to be is a compact pair of binoculars.

He was glad to get rid of the walkie-talkie. It made him feel self-conscious, and the antenna used to jab him in the eye. No-one ever called him up anyway. Unless Litterdale is suddenly overrun by mobsters, or cash-strapped farmers decide to diversify into cannabis cultivation, there is a tacit agreement that Sam should be left to his own devices. Indeed, the only contact with his Chief Inspector is a monthly phone call, merely to check that Sam is alive, well, and keeping Litterdale's crime figures down. This is fine with Sam, and keeps paperwork to a bare minimum.

These days he fills his little black notebook with observations about the birds and animals he sees. And, with the elastic pulled tight, he can press wild flowers flat in a matter of days. Whenever he licks his pencil, to make notes, he gazes wistfully into the distance. There's always a dreamy, faraway look in his eyes. He wants to find the right words to describe the shapes of clouds. Or the bubbling cry of the curlew. Or the way the early morning light picks out the church spire against the still-shadowed hills.

It's high summer in Litterdale. The sky is a deep and unclouded blue, filled with ecstatic swallows, swifts and martins. Sam gazes skywards with a mixture of envy and awe. Whenever he looks at the glories of nature, he feels humble. Mind you, he could look at a box of stale biscuits and feel humble too. That's the truth about Sam, he's just a humble kind of guy.

✳

AUTUMN

The cricketers of Litterdale are coming to terms with another poor season. There'll be no new silverware this year, to brighten up the optimistically large trophy cabinet behind the bar in the Fox. It's hard to cope with failure. It's harder still to fail at all, since the Litterdale and District Cricket League operates an egalitarian 'everyone gets prizes' policy. It means that most teams in the league end up with something tangible at the end of each season.

Talk of 'silverware' rings a little hollow, however, now that the league's trophy budget is being sliced ever more thinly. Instead of lustrous metal, the trophies are cheap and nasty: just plastic sprayed to look like gold. On top of each one is a figure who either bowls or bats, designed by someone ill-acquainted with human anatomy. The batsman looks like he's throwing a stick for a dog; the bowler appears to be dancing a jig. The gold paint soon peels away; after a few weeks the figures appear not merely deformed, but leprous too.

There are trophies for winners, runners-up, best individual performances and most sportsmanlike team. There are commemorative medallions for plucky losers. There's the 'clubman' award which rewards good-hearted guys who, though useless at cricket, bring other talents to the summer game. Like turning out

---

uncomplainingly every weekend, even though they'll bat last (if at all), never get a bowl and field down at third man where the horseflies are. Or mowing the wicket every Friday night. Or shouting 'drinks all round' on a slow night in the pub.

So it's actually quite an achievement for the Litterdale XI to end up with nothing at all. Maybe this feat deserves a trophy too: 'Most Undistinguished Team'. The plastic figure could be seated, head in hands. Something based on Rodin's statue, 'The Thinker'. 'The Plonker', perhaps. On current form, Litterdale could probably keep the trophy in perpetuity.

Dennis, our team captain, is feeling every one of his fifty-five years. It's not easy leading a team of losers through the annual relegation battle. Most weeks of the year – and especially now, at season's end – he thinks about giving up the game altogether. But whenever he thinks about what else he could be doing with his summer weekends – driving to the supermarket, trimming the hedge and spending quality time with his family – he remembers why he took to bat and ball in the first place. Dennis won't need much persuading to carry on leading his lacklustre troops. For one more season, anyway.

The decision won't be his for much longer. On the morning after a particularly hard game, he's just too stiff to roll out of bed. The spirit is willing enough, but the flesh is beginning to weaken. His eyesight isn't what it was either, and he refuses to play in glasses. The price of this vanity is being hit by the ball on a regular basis; this makes his eyes water, so he gets hit even more often. After a long innings his legs look like something out of a Francis Bacon painting: 'Batsman Screaming', perhaps.

Dennis sat in the pub, with the rest of the team, after the penultimate game of the summer, nursing a pint through another pointless session of post-match analysis. They may not shine at cricket, but the members of the Litterdale XI are dab hands at rewriting recent history. To hear them talk, you'd think they'd won the game. Dennis, however, is lost in thought. Time's winged chariot may not be here yet, but he's spotted it coming over the horizon and it's heading his way.

The ageing process starts almost imperceptibly, then picks up speed. As he removes another grey hair from the lapel of his jacket, he mentally lists some of the tell-tale signs. At parties you don't try to chat up the available talent, you just hope you don't get stuck in a low chair. You tune into Radio 2 and find they're playing all your favourite songs. Young people stop being 'us' and start being 'them'.

Your conversations are peppered with meaningless refrains like, 'When I was your age...', 'Of course, that was a lot of money in those days...' and 'You know, perhaps Mary Whitehouse was right after all'. You are tempted by small-ads for sensible trousers in the tabloid papers. You develop an unaccountable interest in golf, gardening and church architecture. You get into the habit of making a milky drink before bedtime. You think twice before buying a five-year diary. Yes, it's disturbing.

There will no doubt come a day when Dennis will spend his Sunday afternoons mooching round a garden centre, but not for a while yet. The problem is that he loves his cricket. Unlike most love affairs, however, his passion becomes more intense as the years slip by. What started out as a mere pastime has developed into a magnificent obsession.

We know all about 'blue collar workers' and 'white collar workers'. But Dennis belongs to a third category, 'open collar workers'. He's an informal dresser, and hates getting dressed up for business meetings. He believes, sensibly enough, that ties restrict the supply of oxygen to the brain. There's only one uniform he enjoys wearing, and that's the one he's wearing today. White flannels, flapping loosely in the breeze, a freshly-ironed cotton shirt and, since there's an autumnal nip in the air, two sweaters. It's the last game of the season, being played under skies of pewter grey, so the broad-brimmed hat is not strictly necessary. Dennis just wouldn't feel dressed without it.

Being next man in, he's following the game closely. One false shot by either of the opening pair, and Dennis will be pulling on his batting gloves. He's got mixed emotions: one part apprehension to two parts exhilaration. The perfect combination. It's possible he may get the same sort of buzz from mowing the lawn or trimming the hedge. Possible... but somehow we doubt it.

Like so many other Peakland communities, Litterdale has had to change with the times. To see how the village looked a hundred years ago, you really ought to catch the exhibition of old photographs that's currently on display in the Tourist Information Centre. Shot during the two decades either side of Queen Victoria's death, these sepia-toned prints offer a beguiling glimpse into a world that, though only three generations away, already seems infinitely and achingly distant.

The pictures were the handiwork of one Archbold Quinlan, local worthy and keen amateur photographer. Though born into a wealthy family, he soon wearied of the pursuits traditionally enjoyed by men of his class, such as riding to hounds, seducing kitchen maids and sending game-birds to meet their maker with his father's shotguns. As he yawned his way through the tedium of interminable country-house parties, he longed to be doing something more useful with his leisure hours.

Photography was an eminently suitable pastime for a man of inherited means, with time hanging heavily on his hands. To be able to capture moments of life, instantly and indelibly, seemed to him utterly magical. Once he had converted part of the hall's old stable block into a darkroom, Quinlan began to train his camera on the immediate surroundings. His family despaired of him; his friends wondered about his sanity. To no avail. He'd found his purpose – his focus, you could say – and nothing would deflect him from it.

It is thanks to energetic and mildly eccentric men like Quinlan that we have such an evocative archive of photographs, showing what life was like before the Great War left the fabric of British life so torn and tattered. He photographed feasts and fairs, high days and holidays, festivals and fêtes. He was there with his camera for Queen Victoria's jubilees, when the village was garlanded with bunting. He caught, on unwieldly glass plates, the mood of heady euphoria when

Mafeking was relieved. Best of all, however, he didn't merely concentrate on the recreations of the idle rich, like some photographic dilettantes of his acquaintance. He focused the bellows of his folding wooden camera, instead, on everyday life in Litterdale.

It's fascinating to see what the village looked like on those days when the flags *weren't* flying: unheralded occasions when sober Litterdale folk were simply going about their business. So let's have a wander around the exhibition, before the prints disappear back into the archive: a collection of cardboard boxes stacked up in the broom cupboard.

Here's a picture of the hardware shop: a crowded emporium that stocked just about everything our great grandparents could possibly need. A handle for a yard brush. A length of chicken wire. Nails and screws sold by the pound. The shopkeeper, wearing a straw hat at a jaunty angle, seems rather pleased with himself. Business looks good. He is happily unaware that, a century later, his establishment would be transformed into a gift shop where tourists browse listlessly for tawdry souvenirs.

A boy and his pig stand in a dusty roadway, both looking towards the camera with studied indifference. Neither of them seem in any great hurry to move. There's no good reason why they should; another dozen years would have passed before the first motor car passed through Litterdale.

Litterdale used to have a village idiot, and here he is: the proud owner of a bewildered expression and an extravagent set of mutton-chop whiskers. Having won the North Derbyshire Village Idiot Competition three years in a row, he got to keep the trophy. Village idiocy is rather out of fashion these days – gone the way of the workhouse and the lunatic asylum. Now, with political correctness to the fore, we have a more humane attitude towards the cerebrally challenged. Yes, Care in the Community, or 'sleeping rough' as it's more accurately known.

The Vicar of Litterdale stands outside the porch of his church. The cut of his frock-coat matches the severity of his countenance. He doesn't look like a man in whom you would confide anything more personal than your collar size. By all accounts he could terrify his congregation with a few home truths delivered from the pulpit – leaving women weeping, men ashen-faced, children traumatised and damp. But, of course, this was a time when religion was a rather more compelling force than it is today. A time when the devil walked among us, and wasn't just your dad dressed up. Before hellfire and damnation had become mere lifestyle options. Before the Ten Commandments had been downgraded to the status of performance charters.

The village blacksmith pays no heed to the photographer. Captured in the process of shoeing a burly carthorse, he has other things on his mind. Like keeping his toes well away from those massive hooves. Anyway, he was unimpressed by photography and other such short-lived fads. He knew that as long as we needed to get from A to B, we would need horses; and as long as we kept horses they would need shoeing. Sadly, he was still repeating this mantra when the first car eventually *did* career through Litterdale – raising dust, frightening livestock and changing the face of transport irrevocably. The blacksmith took early retirement (he didn't have much choice in the matter), and spent his declining years bemoaning the invention of the internal combustion engine.

The smithy, remarkably, has a new lease of life. It was recently saved from dereliction by a college professor who, having taken early retirement, decided to spend his declining years producing hanging baskets and ornate candle-sticks for the tourist trade. Isn't it strange the way things work out?

A vanished way of life is preserved in the aspic of Archbold Quinlan's captivating photographs. They transport us back to what we fondly imagine was a rural arcadia, a pastoral paradise. Not strictly true, of course, but that's the power that sepia-toned photographs can have on our jaded sensibilities at the fag-end of the twentieth century.

❦

Nostalgia is an easy game to play. We can remember, or simply imagine, a Golden Age. Being an essentially meaningless concept, this can be any time in the past: Ancient Greece, the Rennaisance, the Swinging Sixties, a week last Wednesday. It really doesn't matter.

It was a beguiling time, whenever it was. Unicorns roamed the earth, people knew their neighbours, the summers were long and warm, the kids had respect for their elders, working people did a fair day's work for a fair day's pay, and beer was fourpence a pint. They were simpler days, when people knew their place in the scheme of things; we could walk the streets without fear, and pop next door to borrow a cupful of money.

We could leave our front doors unlocked back then, without any bother. We'd keep them open all night. When we went on holiday we'd leave notes for the burglars, telling them the house would be empty for a fortnight. We left explicit instructions about where they could find the valuables; sometimes we'd even go to the trouble of placing a small-ad. in the *Litterdale Times*. But did we ever get burgled? Did we buggery...

There comes a time in life when the world seems to be spinning too quickly on its axis, when the desire to learn new things diminishes along with our eyesight and libidos. And, once we stop learning, the temptation is to take refuge in the past. We bore friends and neighbours with a mantra of memories: farthings, florins, fahrenheit and fuzzy felt. Antirrhinums, antimacassars and avoirdupois. Dubbin and dolly blue. Green Shield stamps, twin-tubs, tiger nuts, spanish, singing cowboys, coltsfoot rock, barley sugar twists, temperance hotels, sarsaparilla, sweet cigarettes (what a great idea *they* were... introducing kids to two lifelong addictions – sugar and nicotine – for the price of one), ginger beer, lemon curd, lead soldiers, penny plain and tuppence coloured.

When logic lets us down, we simplify. Life used to be good, yes it did, but now everything is bad. Childhood memories develop a golden bloom. We were young, untroubled and still had most of our marbles. Unlike now when, if it's quiet, we can actually hear those brain cells popping. It sounds like idle fingers bursting bubble wrap.

Nostalgia can strike anyone, anytime. By any yardstick, Bob's still a young man. Although, if you catch him just after lunch, when he's finished his rounds, you might not think so. He has one of those reclining chairs that, with a casual flick of a lever, transfers a weary postman from a prim, upright sitting position to a relaxed, luxurious sprawl. Within minutes he's asleep and snoring – sporadic twitches in his legs the only clue that savage, untethered dogs are invading his dreams.

By the time the kids get home from school, Bob's up and about again. He knows, from painful experience, that kids and an afternoon nap go together like oil and water. 'Shhh, your dad's asleep,' Cath used to say, as Ben and Sophie burst through the door. But she'd give them a conspiratorial wink too, so the kids would leap onto his chest and pummel him back to consciousness rather quicker than he would have wanted.

The kids are older now. They no longer want to wrestle with dad on the living room floor, more's the pity, or ride on his back like a horse. It doesn't matter what he says to them these days; their only response is to roll their eyes. They head for their rooms, to read magazines, go for a personal best on some shoot-'em-up computer game, or play their music. Loud. Too loud. 'They treat this house like a hotel,' says Bob to Cath. 'It's just the age,' she replies, soothingly. 'They'll get through it. And so will you.' Bob's not so sure.

He claps his hands over his ears. The bass notes from Ben's CD player make his fillings rattle; flakes of plaster fall from the ceiling like an unseasonal flurry of snow. The whole house seems to shake, and not in a good way. Bob takes the stairs two at a time and hammers on his son's bedroom door. 'Turn it down...' 'What?' 'Turn... that... music... down.' Ben glares, but obliges. 'It's giving me a headache,' says Bob, wearily. 'That,' says Ben, coldly, 'is what it's for.' Teenagers...

'That's not music,' Bob says, 'that's just a noise.' He hears himself talking, but the picture that forms in his mind is of his own dad – balding, embattled, uncomprehending – saying those very same words twenty years earlier, as Bob cranked up the volume on his treasured Dansette record player. It's a shock to the system when a man announces (for the first time in his life, but probably not the last) just how much better things were in the good old days. Bob realises, with a crushing certainty, that he is turning into his dad. And not in a good way.

It may be November but Bob, for one, has a spring in his step. As he hoists the postbag over one shoulder (years of delivering letters have left him a little lop-sided), he sniffs the air. There's a heady mixture: the musty scent of fallen leaves mingling with pungent bonfire smoke. He counts his blessings too. He's got a wife who puts up with his failings and foibles. He's got two bright kids who may deign, one day, to have a two-way conversation with him. In five years' time he'll have paid off the mortgage. Yes, things aren't what they used to be. They're a hell of a lot better…

WINTER

From the vantage point of a Peakland village, the whole world seems to be going barking mad. There's an air of near-hysteria, like a kid who can't wait to open the pile of Christmas presents. There's a mounting sense of pointlessness, too, like one of those crazy farm-dogs that runs around in circles, trying to catch its own tail. Yes, for months we've all been whipped into a frenzy of anticipation about the millennium, and what a good time we're all going to have. But there's only so long you can sustain such a level of breathless hype. And now, as we round the final bend in the last lap of the old millennium, we've crossed the boredom threshold. Here in Litterdale, at least, we've had enough.

The landlords of the Swan and the Fox have been rubbing their hands together, as they plan how to spend all the money they reckon they'll take over New Year. Trade in the old car, perhaps, or take a much-needed break. A proper holiday, not just a day at a brewers' trade show. They're hoping to keep their customers in an amiably spendthrift mood for what is expected to be about seventy-two straight hours of drinking and merrymaking.

The Fox is the village's workaday drinking hole: no airs, no graces, no locks on the toilet door. No dress-code either; most of the customers are men who tuck their shirts into their underpants. The landlord – a large man with a face like a beef tomato – is focusing on the youth market, and will be offering a variety of unsophisticated entertainments. He plans to kick off Millennium Eve with a special trivia quiz. In deference to the pub's customers, who are mostly from the shallow end of the gene pool, the questions will be untaxing. Like: 'Who are *you* looking at?' 'Wanna make something of it?' The prize will be a platter of raw meat – not so much a mixed grill as an autopsy.

The Vinnie Jones lookalike contest, pencilled in for later in the evening, might not prove, in retrospect, to have been the brightest idea the landlord's ever had. The after-midnight car-door slamming competition, held in the car-park, is a regular feature in the pub's social calendar. The customers can be entrusted to sort out the running order for themselves.

The landlord at the Swan has no plans for such plebeian pastimes to usher in the new millennium. This is Litterdale's self-styled 'nice pub for nice people', where a new flavour of crinkle-cut crisp is usually reckoned to be excitement enough for his more upmarket clientele. To mark the millennium, however, the landlord is busy creating a brand new menu. A French menu: well, French in the way that *'Allo 'Allo* is French.

It may look like easy money for the licensees of Litterdale, but there's a fly in the ointment. No, not the bug we've heard so much about. The main problem is getting the staff to work at all on Millennium Eve. They've been whispering in conspiratorial huddles, plucking ever-larger sums of money out of the air, just to hear how good they sound. For this one-off occasion, at least, the workers reckon to have the bosses over a barrel. Only now, after weeks of haggling, have the landlords and their staff reached agreement. Those who turn out on that special day will get five times their usual pay, in return for a moratorium on spitting in the soup until the New Year holiday is well and truly over.

Will the rest of us have any 'mad money' left to spend on Millennium Eve, once Christmas has taken its toll on our credit cards and mental equilibrium? The question has been answered already, as we scan the last page of our calendars. We're busy cancelling those millennium parties. A quiet night in, doing a crossword, has never looked more appealing.

Those prepared to drive into town – and leave their critical faculties at home – will be able to see a Christmas pantomime. Probably starring one of the gladiators (Ferret), a monosyllabic Rugby League star with no neck, the straight man in a now-defunct comedy duo, and an actress who was booted out of some TV soap back in 1987. A mouth-watering prospect, no doubt, though live entertainment can also be found even closer to home.

The Litterdale Strollers, our local amateur dramatic company, have been striving manfully to give us quality theatre. God only knows why they bother; to date we've shown ourselves to be stubbornly resistant to the lure of the classics. Two years ago, for example, the company staged *King Lear*. It was an ambitious production, by all accounts, but not even the overly-realistic eye-gouging scene could fill more than half the seats in the village hall. Living in Pennine Derbyshire we already know what it's like to bring up ungrateful kids in adverse weather conditions.

Last Christmas the Strollers put on a musical, hoping that a medley of undemanding melodies would pull in the punters. *Don't Cry For Me, Arthur Negus* was a heartwarming tale of life, love and laughter at the sharp end of the antiques business. There was a glowing review in the *Litterdale Times*: 'You'll laugh, you'll cry... you'll rifle your granny's attic for items of more than sentimental value.' Word of mouth did the rest; the last night's performance was almost a sell-out.

The Strollers have gone back to the bard for this year's offering too, but this time they've given one of his best-loved plays what they hope will be a crowd-pleasing twist. *All's Well That Tideswell* is a triumphant reworking of Shakespeare's play in a contemporary Peakland setting. We're hoping it will bring Litterdale folk out in droves, and break all box-office records.

The whole millennium scenario has proved less than contagious here in Litterdale. Millennium fever? Millennium torpor, more like. While the travel agents were trying to persuade us to spend the first morning of the new millennium in some sun-kissed holiday paradise, we didn't really care where we'd be... as long as it wasn't a place where we'd have to rely on computers and microchips. So not 30,000 feet up in a doomed jumbo jet, if you please, or hooked up to some crucial life-support machine.

The millennium scenario was strangely familiar; Litterdale's more anxious citizens had replayed it many times in their feverish imaginations... The clock chimes twelve on the last night of the old year. Digital timers click fatefully from 1999 into the uncharted territory that is the year 2000. Computers implode, instantly. Irreplaceable data disappears into the ether, never to be seen again. Household appliances go berserk. Savings and investments evaporate; the FT index drops through the floor; we're reduced to bartering with beads. Within seconds we're back in the Middle Ages, the fabric of society unravelling like a badly-knitted sweater.

That was the worst-case scenario, at least if you listened to the merchants of doom who were prepared, at a price, to rid our computers of those pesky millennium bugs. They presented a Shakespearean vision of global meltdown: sour, stinging winds; plagues of boils; birds singing out of tune; the seasons blending into one, an endless winter. But they *would* say that, wouldn't they?

As unpleasant as these predictions sounded, there was an alternative possibility so terrifying that no-one dared even to consider it. What if *nothing* untoward happened on that fateful day? What if everything was the same as it was before? Just another day. Just another dollar. The familiar routine: five days of meaningless labour, with only beer and telly to ease the pain, followed by a weekend of ploughing listlessly through a pile of Sunday supplements.

What if aeroplanes kept flying, toasters worked perfectly and computers continued to spew out specious nonsense? We'd be feeling rather silly on the morning after those 'what the hell, we're all going to die' millennium parties. Adulterous couples creeping out of lustful beds, red-faced and chastened, to face the music from their respective spouses. Disgruntled employees begging to have their job back, having unwisely told the boss, the week before, exactly where he could stick it. Now *that* was the nightmare scenario...

Scoop, the editor of the *Litterdale Times*, has remained commendably level-headed throughout the past few months, refusing to succumb to millennium madness. Idle 'end of the world' speculation would only have encouraged more readers to cancel their subscriptions, and an ailing newspaper needs all the readers it can muster. He knows that every new year is special, and that the year 2000 will prove no exception. But beyond that it's all just numbers, with no more significance than, say, the mileometer on his elderly Austin Princess ticking over from 99,999 miles – as it did recently – to 100,000.

As a founder member of CLOC (the Central Lane Owner's Club) Scoop prides himself on being a careful driver. He's owned the car from new, and – as he taps the polished walnut-style fascia for luck – he maintains that in all those years it's never had so much as a scratch. That's probably because he cruises myopically along at a stately 30mpm, like minor royalty, with a queue of impatient motorists building up behind. Lost in a flatulent fug, humming along to a Gilbert and Sullivan operetta, he remains blissfully unaware of the strong feelings he inspires in other road-users: apoplectic rage, mostly. It always comes as a surprise to Scoop to see angry drivers overtake – often on blind bends, raising a hail of gravel – their knuckles white from gripping the steering wheel too tightly.

Scoop had been keeping a watchful eye on the mileometer throughout the 99,990s; after all, it's not every day that a car reaches the milestone of six figures. When the great moment finally arrived, he was deep in thought, composing a banner headline for the next issue. When he glanced back at the dashboard he found he'd missed the moment entirely. The clock read 100,003. His first thought was to put the car into reverse, and try to 'lose' a few miles. But what would have been the point? Once these moments have gone, there's no way to bring them back. They have to be seized, not choreographed.

Which explains why the millennium celebrations have largely failed to enthral the good folk of Litterdale. When there's too much anticipation, and not enough substance, we know we're only heading for disappointment. Here in rural Derbyshire we haven't yet lost touch with the changing of the seasons. We have schedules and calendars of our own, jobs around the farm that can't be postponed merely because the people on TV have been getting over-excited. When there is something genuinely worth celebrating, we don't spend the whole year thinking 'Wow, what a night *that's* going to be.' We don't talk about it, we just do it. Yes, once the last of the new year hangovers has subsided, it looks as though life in Litterdale will soon get back to normal.

The days are short and the nights are long over the course of a Litterdale winter. When the sun seems to go down shortly after lunch, we have plenty of time to mull over some of life's knottier questions. Like why is there a 'best by' date on sour cream? Why don't we have a 99p coin? Just think how useful it would be. Why don't film censors get depraved and corrupt? And whatever happened to the Bermuda Triangle? Back in the 1970s ships and planes were going AWOL every other day. And now it's disappeared. Without warning. Weird.

Rain hammers down incessantly on our Peakland village. It beats on the roof-tiles, like the drumming of impatient fingers, and bounces off the roads. Water pulsates over unswept gutters and sluices down unpointed walls, turning stone-flagged yards into slippery skid-pans. Fluorescent green moss grows luxuriantly in dank, forgotten corners, creating tiny ecosystems where pale, sightless creatures wait, with infinite forbearance, to take over the world.

The river that runs beneath the twin arches of the old packhorse bridge is transformed into an angry torrent. Wood, swept down from the hills by flood-water, piles up in a disorderly log-jam against the stone stanchions. Scraps of paper lodge in the branches of overhanging trees, and flutter like Tibetan prayer-flags. Mallards shoot the rapids, spinning like corks in the eddies and whirlpools.

It may be wet, but it's not that cold. Not like Litterdale used to be. Older villagers can remember winters when the village was almost buried beneath stowering snow. Sometimes it drifted so deep that they couldn't open their front doors, and had to climb out of upstairs windows instead.

The last really hard winter we had was fifteen years ago, when the village was cut off for days. Thanks to a bout of panic-buying by our more anxious residents, the village shop soon ran short of fresh food. We had to make do with whatever we could find, which meant a monotonous diet of snack noodles for breakfast, lunch and dinner. We soon came to realise that pouring boiling water into a plastic pot does not, after all, transform a mixture of brick-dust and E-numbers into a tasty and nutritional meal. The only people who got through the experience unscathed were the bachelor farmers. They eat pot snacks from choice, thus enabling them to make washing up a manageable once-a-year chore.

Thanks to global warming, hard winters have probably gone for ever. Heavy snow is uncommon enough nowadays to warrant a headline in the *Litterdale Times*. Some years we just get the lightest of snowfalls that leave the tiled roofs of our little houses looking like they've been dusted with icing sugar.

Most of us are happy to have warmer winters. But not all. Our local undertaker, for example, has time unexpectedly on his hands. A frock-coated vulture, he sits morosely at the bar of the Swan, trying to drown his sorrows. As callous as it may seem to those outside this noble profession, he's worried that the mild winters aren't killing off old people in the accustomed numbers. He'd only gone into the funeral business on the understanding that he'd never be short of work. God knows there aren't too many other perks; none that he'll admit to, anyway.

Business is bad. The old folk of Litterdale seem depressingly sprightly. Spring is almost here, and if we don't get some late snow, or at least a hard frost, he'll be forced to lay off staff. He's only trying to make an honest living, but not everyone shares his idiosyncratic views. He wrote a letter to the paper, suggesting that our senior citizens could give the local economy a much-needed boost simply by turning their central heating down by a few degrees. It didn't seem much to ask, yet he's been getting hate-mail ever since. Someone should take him to one side and tell him to forget that 'two for the price of one' offer, as well, before he upsets the whole village. He's losing his grip; maybe he's been in the funeral business too long.

While most folk in Litterdale can see no further than the next rainy day, Bill, our tourism officer, is already dreaming of long summer days. It's his remit to persuade people to spend some of their leisure hours and spending money in and around the valley. To this end he's putting the finishing touches to a glossy new brochure aimed at getting holiday-makers to think: 'Hmmm, Litterdale, that sounds like the place for me.'

During the winter months, Bill has attended some marketing seminars: confrontational days full of sales stratagems, brand awareness and team-building exercises. After all that positive dynamism, it was quite a relief to get back to the relative peace and quiet of his little office in Litterdale. If Bill has learned anything from these gatherings, it's the need to identify, and then ruthlessly exploit, Litterdale's 'unique selling points'.

Maybe we're biased, but we think the valley has just about everything that makes life worth living. Since the stage-coaches stopped running, Litterdale has become a pleasant little backwater, not really on the way to anywhere. And if the local farmers delight in misdirecting lost motorists, well, let's be charitable and suggest that it's a perk of an increasingly stressful job. But we don't have a spectacular waterfall, or show-caves, or a museum devoted to sculptures made entirely of ear wax. In truth, the attraction of Litterdale is that it isn't so special. It's homely, comfortable and welcoming, the touristic equivalent of a fireside rug and a mug of

Horlicks. Visitors know what they're going to find ('A view, a brew and a loo', as Bill acknowledges in one of his more cynical moments) and they all seem to go home happy. It won't be too long before the first visitors arrive, and our love/hate relationship will begin again.

SPRING

It's Spring in Litterdale and the sap is rising. Young men think of love, or lust, or at least a hot date for Saturday night. Mother Nature is showing the way, by giving us the birds and bees as role models. Okay, bees may be conspicuous by their absence, but the birds, at least, are busy building their nests. Blue tits investigate nooks and crannies. Rooks make running repairs to the same wind-tossed, tree-top nests they've used for years. Jackdaws display either stupidity or the patience of Job, by dropping twigs down chimney pots. Sooner or later one twig will lodge in the flue, and a second and a third, to provide a platform to support a nest (and, for the householder, a hearth full of twigs).

You can almost hear the hum of testosterone, as young lads, wreathed in clouds of cheap cologne, try to impress the local lasses with feats of strength. Yes, love may make the world go round, but it's lust that lubricates the moving parts.

Litterdale's senior citizens, in contrast, have largely come to terms with their waning powers, with no more than a shrug of the shoulders and the occasional twinge of regret on seeing a well-turned ankle. In the lottery of love they've long since cashed in their chips. The flame of passion burns less brightly as the years slip by;

sometimes the pilot light goes out altogether. The old folks look elsewhere for excitement these days: a cup of weak tea, a trip to the garden centre, another punt on some hopeless nag in the 2.30 at Wincarnis.

Norman's at that difficult age, when a man has to prioritise. Should he continue his search for a relationship more meaningful than that between a man and his newsagent? Is it realistic now to hope for the love of a good woman, or should he just bow to the inevitable and settle instead for the companionship of a gerbil?

At three o'clock in the afternoon, on a chilly March day, Litterdale's football team is being cheered onto the muddy pitch by a few loyal fans. So few, indeed, that the team has been informed, over the tannoy, of changes to the crowd. The spectators blow on their hands, for warmth, and rub them together. Older guys test the credulity of the younger fans by recalling the Ice Age ('Now that *was* cold...') when the Arctic weather brought such chaos to the fixture list that the pools panel had to meet for three million Saturdays in a row.

Litterdale Rovers are known in the league – the Vauxhall Cars Beezer Homes Sherpa Van Division (North) – as a sleeping dwarf. The manager – it's just Norman in a camel-hair coat – had to take drastic action to turn the season around. When he swapped the entire squad for two bags of Cheesy Wotsits, footballing pundits reckoned he'd got the best of the bargain.

The new crop of players have mostly been plucked from park football. Still unaccustomed to the luxury of real goalposts they have to be dissuaded from throwing their jackets down on the grass before the start of play. The captain picks his team in traditional fashion ('one potato, two potato...') which is why the scrawny players with glasses warm the substitutes' benches for game after game.

When the sports reporter from the *Litterdale Times* – it's just Scoop in a deerstalker hat – says that the players are 'a good advertisement for the game', he is merely pointing out that they are covered from head to foot in sponsors' logos. Norman is trying to adopt the system of man-to-man marketing that has served Derby County so well. The team's strip is now being sponsored, appropriately enough, by a local knacker's yard. To the question 'How's the team performing?' there's only one answer: 'Offal'. Whenever they get injured, the players are contracted to crawl in front of an advertising hoarding, in case the photographer from the *Litterdale Times* has remembered to put a film in his camera. Yes, the financial situation at the club really is that dire.

Norman likes to use a bit of sports psychology, to boost his players' motivation. Nevertheless, when it comes to getting the required result, no-one's yet come up with a better strategy than locking the players in a small room for twenty minutes and hurling abuse at them. The church bells are chiming three o'clock, so the talking has to stop. Before taking his place on the bench, Norman cups his hands and bellows his final encouragement: 'The grass is green, the paint is fresh... so get out there and bloody play.'

New arrivals in Litterdale always attract attention. Whether we're neighbourly, or just plain nosy, is open to question. No matter, we'll accept any excuse to extend the hand of friendship, and check out the newcomers' taste in soft furnishings.

We were flabbergasted when Primrose Cottage found a buyer. It had been standing empty for years, due to a catalogue of structural defects, and every year that passed only made it less likely to sell. It had been on the market for so long that the 'For Sale' sign had almost disappeared beneath an exuberant growth of ivy. The winter winds had loosened roof-slates; leaf-choked gutters had started to sag like a saddle-backed horse. The front garden, once a colourful profusion of lupins and hollyhocks, had become over-run with weeds.

Primrose Cottage has oodles of what the estate agent calls 'character'. The villagers, with a more prosaic turn of phrase, prefer 'semi-derelict'. You wouldn't touch the place with a six-foot barge-pole... unless you wanted to be the proud owner of a six-foot barge-pole with dry rot. Convinced that there's a mug born every minute, the vendor continued to bide his time. So it seemed like Christmas had come early when Mandy arrived in Litterdale and immediately fell in love with the place. Love is blind, a condition that's not improved by wearing rose-coloured glasses.

Mandy has a trusting nature, and she doesn't like to be on the receiving end of bad news. The surveyor's report made such depressing reading that she threw it straight in the bin. She backed her feminine intuition instead, which proved to be an expensive mistake. As pretty as it is, Primrose Cottage is a black hole of a house; it could suck in as much money as anyone would think of throwing at it, and still be barely habitable. But Mandy had a warm feeling about the house; it had a welcoming aura. All it needed, she reckoned, was a lick of paint, a wind-chime and a few house plants. A recent divorce settlement had left her with money to spend, so she bought the place for cash. Unfortunately, that warm feeling turned out to be nothing more than heartburn.

Mandy and her daughter moved into Primrose Cottage, thus beginning a battle with subsidence and rotting timbers that has continued ever since. It's what can happen when you take decisions based on something as insubstantial as the turn of a tarot card or the juxtaposition of the planets. Mandy, you see, is a new-age believer; she's ransacked the wisdom of the East to assemble a pick-and-mix portfolio of irrationality.

She missed the explicit warnings in the surveyor's report, despite them being flagged up with a fluorescent highlighter pen. Yet she's happy to espouse any old mumbo-jumbo, as long as it's dressed up in Eastern robes. The more unlikely the better. She's a big fan of Feng Shui, the ancient art of creating harmony in our homes. Why bother wrestling with the questions that have taxed mankind for centuries, when all we need to do, apparently, is to rearrange the furniture? Some directives seem obvious. Don't use a powerful Hoover near a long-haired dog. Get rid of those unsightly piles of Feng Shui books that are cluttering up the place. And if none of this stuff works there's always the English version of Feng Shui, which consists of tidying up.

With evangelical conviction, Mandy is trying to introduce some of her new-age ideas to the good folk of Litterdale. Having perused half a dozen *Readers Digest* articles on topics as wide-ranging as reflexology, past-life regression and knitting with dog hair, she feels eminently qualified to enlighten us.

Litterdale is a traditional kind of place, and the new-age phenomenon has largely passed us by. We don't rush to embrace every new fad and fashion, like they do in town. Most of the villagers wouldn't know whether shiatsu was a massage technique or a breed of cat. Some of us are only just coming to terms with decimal currency and pain-free dentistry. It's not that we're necessarily resistant to change. And we're not immune to gullibility either. After all, a recent pyramid-selling scam only faltered when every villager was trying to sell overpriced household detergents to everybody else.

Yes, we'd like to believe in all this new-age claptrap, we really would. It's tempting to believe that our misfortunes might be due to celestial alignments, rather than our own fecklessness. But the fact is that we have a more pragmatic approach to reading the future. We have the weather forecast, of course, and we can learn a lot from perusing the auction prices. In any case, the farmers have a pretty good idea what they'll be doing tomorrow, and the day after, and the day after that... because it'll be much the same as what they did yesterday.

The good folk of Litterdale are baffled when Mandy presses one of her pastel-coloured business cards ('Meaningless affirmations, your place or mine') into their reluctant hands. It's mildly disconcerting to hear about other worlds, distant galaxies and alternative realities, especially from a woman who has difficulties reading a road-map. We'd think twice before making an appointment for a tarot card reading with Mandy, in the same way that we'd think twice before hiring the services of a fingerless carpenter.

Genuine evidence of Mandy's powers of clairvoyance are not easy to find. And, let's face it, we're willing to be convinced. Advance notification of those six lottery numbers would make a convincing start. But Mandy gets crotchety when her powers of foresight are questioned. 'Look, I can just *sense* these things, all right?'

It's good to see the smoke curling lazily from the chimneys of Primrose Cottage once again, and we hope that Mandy will settle to life in the village. We hope, too, that she'll find a few paying customers for her brand of oven-ready platitudes; it looks like she'll be needing the money.

Down at Litterdale's compact cricket ground, Dennis is marshalling his troops for yet another assault on the league title. Following last season's disappointment at collecting the wooden spoon, he has made some dramatic changes to the personnel. Now, having brought in seven new players, he reckons he's only three men short of a half-decent team.

Dennis wants to deliver his traditional pre-game pep-talk, so the team has convened in the pavilion. That's what we call it, though it's actually just a shabby pile of breeze-blocks and chipboard, with all the architectural allure of an allotment shed. It's been put together, over the years, in piecemeal fashion – sprouting another lean-to annexe whenever we needed somewhere to keep the mower, make tea, or site a rudimentary toilet. If we carried on building in this way, we'd soon have a shanty town.

The roller stays outside, padlocked to a tree. If anyone wants to go to the trouble of stealing it, they're very welcome. It's big, heavy and almost seized up with rust. We're sick of the sight of it. We've pushed the damned thing up and down the pitch for years, to no apparent effect. Despite our best efforts, the wicket is as unpredictable as ever. Batsmen don't know whether the next ball will whistle past their ears or shoot along the ground. Batting can be an excruciating business.

Dennis crosses his legs gingerly as he thinks back to when he acquired his first cricket protector. He was just a lad, glad to be getting a game or two for the team, but embarrassed to be stuffing a folded-up copy of the *Daily Mirror* down his trousers before he went in to bat. He paid a visit to the sports shop in town, but became flustered on finding a woman behind the counter. Tongue-tied and red-faced, Dennis gesticulated towards a display cabinet with one hand, and proffered a clammy palmful of small change with the other. He left, hurriedly, with the cheapest cricket box in the shop. It proved to be a false economy; the few pennies he saved almost cost him his manhood.

It was shaped like half an avocado pear (the box, that is, not his manhood) and was moulded in pink plastic. The viciously sharp, unpadded edges should have made Dennis think twice before parting with his pocket money. However, it wasn't until he faced some seriously fast bowling that the box's deficiencies became painfully apparent. A direct hit with a cricket ball had the same effect on Dennis's groin (I'll put it as delicately as I can) that a pastry-cutter has when pushed into freshly-kneaded dough. Forty years on, the memory can still bring tears to his eyes and a flush to his cheeks.

There's a poisonous atmosphere in the cricket pavilion today: a heady pot-pourri of sweat, fungus, unwashed socks, cheap deodorant, horse liniment, athletes foot lotion, talcum powder, mildew, hand-rolled tobacco and unrestrained flatulence. It's gloomy too; the grubby windows are shrouded with spiders' webs, where the trussed-up corpses of unwary flies are marinating gently. A prawn salad sandwich, thoughtlessly abandoned under a bench last September, is giving off a pale phosphorescent glow. Scientists seeking the perfect conditions for the propagation of virulent bacteria need look no further than Litterdale's premier sporting facility.

The cricket hut is essentially a masculine environment. Women, even those blessed with strong constitutions, would no sooner cross the threshold on match days than wear jam in their hair. In any case the wives and girlfriends of the Litterdale XI have better things to do with their leisure hours than watch a bunch of overweight men chase a red ball around a field.

It was different in the old days. There used to be an inexhaustible supply of good-hearted women in the village who'd be only too happy to make sandwiches, bake scones and mash the tea. To compensate for the inevitable bruises, visiting teams knew there would always be a good spread whenever they came to Litterdale. Nowadays, alas, the players have to do everything themselves. It means that 'tea' is nothing more than a catering pack of salt and vinegar crisps and a few debilitating cans of industrial-strength lager.

No matter; the sun is shining today on Litterdale's cricket ground, and the players are easing themselves into the new season with a strict regime of isometric inertia. The only member of the team who loosens up before a game is our wicket-keeper; he's the only one with muscles. As he straps neoprene supports around creaking elbows and knees, he appears to be built out of spare parts from a breaker's yard.

While the rest of the team sit around drinking beer and cadging roll-ups, he performs inelegant and painful-looking callisthenics. Consequently he is the only one who ever gets injured before the game: a regular litany of sprains and pulls, requiring yet more liniment and support garments. It's a downward spiral of exercise, injury and visits to the surgical supplies shop that will end, to no one's great surprise, with him falling to bits altogether.

The smell of new-mown grass has the same effect on club cricketers as a boat of steaming gravy has on the Bisto Kids. It makes us close our eyes, adopt angelic expressions and sniff the air. You only need to look at the paunches on display to realise that the members of the Litterdale XI still have an appetite for the game. Or maybe just an appetite. The first swallows are here, so we know that summer can't be far behind. Following Dennis's inspirational team-talk the players take to the field with confidence: a confidence that lasts right up to the moment that the umpire says 'Play' and a new season gets underway.

SUMMER

Everyone has their favourite time of the year, and in a straw poll there would be plenty of votes for autumnal tints, an old-fashioned Christmas and the candyfloss colours of springtime blossom. But early summer would get my vote. A warm, balmy June day is, I would suggest, about as good as the English climate gets. The Litterdale landscape looks serene. The first five months of the year are just dress rehearsals for this; yes, June is the finished article.

The more irritating members of the insect world have yet to muster in numbers. And even the grumpiest of our senior citizens won't begin to complain about the heat for another fortnight. It will be at least a month before the greens in the landscape lose their vivid intensity. Two months before the hay is gathered in, and the Peakland scene is redrawn in desiccated sepia tones. For now, though, we walk around in shirt-sleeves, enjoying the sunshine and the cottage gardens bursting with flowers.

Bill is reviewing all his strategies for attracting visitors to the area. As slogans go, 'Come to Litterdale, You'll Like It' is beginning to look a little lame. He sucks the end of his pencil, in search of inspiration, and stares at the ceiling. He's looking for the holy grail of tourism: a slogan so meaningless and enigmatic that it will attract visitors in droves. Suddenly the light bulb above his head comes on and Bill scribbles furiously on the back of an envelope, before settling back in his revolving chair to admire his handiwork. 'Lovely Litterdale, where the present meets the past and makes an elegant swallow dive into the future.' Yes, it's a masterpiece.

In an effort to pad out this year's tourist brochure, Bill looked for any literary connections that Litterdale may have had. But, drawing a blank, he had to kick-start the new campaign with a harmless white lie. Charles Dickens stayed in Litterdale – that's what the brochure says – and he may have written some of his novels here. An intriguing thought, of course, but still only that… a thought. In truth, Charles Dickens came to this little backwater just the once, and merely for a discreet consultation about an embarrassing rash.

That might have marked the end of Bill's career as a teller of tall tales. Except that he's just received a fax from his boss, congratulating him on his skills at unearthing previously unknown facts about Litterdale, and ending up with 'Can we please have some more?' A march of two thousand miles begins with but a single step, so people say. And Bill is taking his first tentative steps down the perfumed path that leads to the eternal bonfire. The trouble with a little white lie is where it leads you.

This is why, on a sunny day in June, Bill is ensconced in Litterdale's lending library, leafing through the books in the 'local history' section. If anything of importance ever happened in the village, he has yet to find any tangible evidence of it. At this rate, he'll have to harness all his powers of imagination, and next year's tourism brochure will be filed under 'fiction'.

The landlord of the Swan rubs his hands together expectantly when he sees carloads of day-trippers descending on the village. He grits his teeth and forces a smile as his pub fills up with noisy kids. Knowing what the mark-up is on a small glass of lemonade, he's prepared to put up with the inconvenience. At the Fox, on the other hand, children aren't welcome until they're tall enough to stand at the bar and buy a round like everybody else. And the only concession to the tourist trade, here at Litterdale's less salubrious alehouse, is a lacklustre campaign to bring back spittoons.

Across the village green, at Primrose Cottage, Mandy is trying to tap into the lucrative bed and breakfast market. Since Litterdale folk seem disinclined to pay for astrological forecasts, she needs the extra money to do repairs on her tumbledown house. It's a heap, frankly; you could double its value simply by screwing a satellite dish to the wall. So Mandy is offering what she calls 'self-centred accommodation', aimed at people so narcissistic that they won't notice the squalor in which she lives. In addition to basic bed and breakfast, she's throwing in a free tarot-card reading.

Primrose Cottage appears in the new accommodation guide, but only as the village's sole representative in the hastily concocted 'cheap and cheerful' section. And Bill couldn't, in all honesty, award the place any stars for service or amenities. Telling bare-faced lies about Litterdale is one thing, but he can't recommend Primrose Cottage to any visitors who aren't up to date with their rabies shots.

Mandy spends so much time meditating that mundane chores remain undone, sometimes for weeks. Meditating is what she calls it, anyway, though to most Litterdale folk it looks more like sitting around, doing nothing. What kind of meditation includes daytime TV? Housework is not Mandy's forté (even her laugh is infectious), and visitors are wise to sniff the milk before they pour it on their organic muesli.

The first thing that guests are likely to see, as they walk inside the house, is an over-laden cat-litter tray. Sensible visitors understand immediately that they've made a big mistake, offer some excuse and make their escape. After five minutes at Mandy's, fresh air never smelled so good. The turmoil even extends beyond her front door. Litterdale's accommodation guide suggests that the garden of Primrose Cottage looks a picture. Sadly, it's a picture by Hieronymous Bosch.

✻

It's July in Litterdale. High summer when, according to that hoary old joke, thousands come here for the solitude. At times this pretty Peakland village can seem unbearably overcrowded. Despite all the best efforts of the National Park Authority to get them to use public transport, visitors are reluctant to leave their cars at home. Inspired, perhaps, by the name of our village, they load up their cars with litter, and leave it here as a souvenir of their visit. Yes, they like to make their presence felt – with the squeal of balding tyres on hot Tarmac and the relentless boom, boom, boom of in-car stereo systems, cranked up to migraine-inducing volume. If they were subjected to this kind of noise during working hours, their shop stewards would be clamouring for compensation.

It seems a little strange to us that so many townies come to Litterdale, ostensibly to escape the noise, clutter and pollution of our northern cities, only to bring their own noise, clutter and pollution with them. But even on the sunniest of summer weekends, when Litterdale is throbbing with visitors, it's easy to escape the crowds. As locals are well aware (and the more discerning visitors, too), the noise quells to an unobtrusive murmur within ten minutes of lacing up the walking boots and taking any of the delightful green lanes that radiate away from the village.

Some people, sadly, find the countryside unnerving. They feel more comfortable with unresponsive concrete beneath their feet. They prefer the regimented rows of streets and houses in an A-Z street atlas to the sinuous curves of the contour lines on an Ordnance Survey map (which, in any case, they can neither read nor fold). The thought of going without such aspects of city life as lottery tickets and southern fried chicken, even for half a day, seems to fill them with a nameless dread. Worst of all, they are convinced they will get hopelessly lost. Yes, landscapes that beckon seasoned walkers can hold a multitude of terrors for townies.

Midsummer is the ideal time to show these benighted souls that the Peakland landscape can be invitingly benign. The grassy slopes and dry stone walls create ever-changing patterns of light and colour that never fail to fascinate. Even when walkers crest a hill, the breeze that brushes their faces is as warm as a kiss. Bare trees aren't being bent by savage winter winds. Blizzards are unlikely. In short, there's little to disturb the most timid of walkers.

The rivers around Litterdale meander unhurriedly through ancient valleys of limestone crags, screes and moss-covered rocks. No wonder Izaak Walton was so enchanted by their clear waters. Sulphur-yellow wagtails chase each other along the water-margins. Dippers slide effortlessly beneath the surface. Startled moorhens skitter into the reeds. Dragonflies flash by: vivid blurs of electric greens and blues. The air is still and soporific. Stand on an old packhorse bridge. Feel the warmth and texture of weathered stone beneath your palms. Gaze down into the water. Watch the waterweed waving, hypnotically, like manes of hair, and trout basking lazily in the shallows. Let your problems melt away; there'll be time enough to deal with them once you get home. Slip into the silence, with the same ease as the dipper, leaving barely a ripple.

There are many kinds of silence. There's the embarrassed silence you get at breakfast in a seaside boarding house, which only makes the tinkling of tea-cups seem deafening by comparison. There's the blissful silence when a car alarm finally drains the battery and whines to a merciful stop. There's the brooding silence at the heart of a marriage when love has died. But best of all are those moments when the chatter of the mind abates, when memories, ambitions and everyday worries evaporate like puddles on a hot pavement, and, however briefly, you are blessed with stillness.

It gets ever harder to hear the silence through the crackle and static of everyday life. We rush through the working week as though it were a race, hardly daring to stop, look and listen, in case – gulp – we discover we've wasted our best years doing something monumentally pointless, like being an estate agent. Then we fill our weekends with so many activities, that leisure, too, begins to resemble work. It seems we're upset by silence. Even when they're not playing Musak, supermarkets routinely broadcast 'white noise': a low hum, like the noise a fridge makes, that puts us into a relaxed, more spendthrift mood.

But the silence in the countryside isn't just an absence of noise. The sweet song of the skylark and the bubbling cry of the curlew are just two of the sounds that don't disrupt the stillness. In contrast, there are quieter sounds that *do*: radios, mobile phones, even the insistent beeping of digital watches – dividing up the hours into convenient chunks for those who believe that most mendacious of equations, that time is money.

Many people spend their free time playing shoot-'em-up computer games, or watching furiously paced films featuring men in dirty vests outrunning fireballs. These people will probably watch more senseless violence in the course of an hour than you'd witness in the taproom of the Fox over, oh, an entire Bank Holiday weekend. And here in Litterdale we can go for weeks without experiencing anything more cataclysmic than a chip-pan fire in the pub's kitchen. People who are over-stimulated, like children who quaff too many fizzy drinks, need bigger and bigger doses of eye-popping sensation. They are unlikely to respond to the quiet lure of the countryside, where excitements are subtle rather than blatant. Where you can stand on a hilltop and gaze across the patchwork of fields to the village you call home.

Can something this beautiful really be the result of a chaotic accident? Just the chance collision of particles all those eons ago? The 'big bang' that movie directors seem so determined to replicate on film. Looking at Litterdale, spread out in the valley like a picnic arranged on a cloth of green gingham, it's not hard to believe that there is, after all, a celestial hand on the tiller.

✱

It's August in Litterdale. We are in the middle of the school holidays when, with weeks still to go before the autumn term begins, parents are already running out of things to keep their kids amused. 'I'm bored' is an oft-heard cry from children whose first act, on waking up to a sunny summer's day, is to switch on the TV for an hour or two of mindless cartoons.

It's not easy being a parent, of course. There's a conspiracy of silence surrounding the whole business. After all, if young couples knew the whole truth about parenting, the human race would die out within a few generations. Some of them imagine that the most painful part of parenting will be stepping on a Lego brick with bare feet. In which case, they'll get a nasty surprise. That's why the process of conceiving babies is designed to be such fun. We are seduced into thinking that child-rearing will, in its own way, be equally rewarding. Our children will be tiny versions of ourselves, we imagine, to whom we can impart all our skills and wisdom. But those few minutes of fun come at a fearful price, as parenting takes its toll, and prove beyond all doubt that God does indeed have a sense of humour.

It's not so easy being a kid either. Men and women can behave pretty irrationally once they become parents. It begins with something just mildly hypocritical like telling their kids to 'Do as I say, not as I do', but it gets weirder. Parents warn children about the dangers of playing with matches. Then, every autumn, explosives are openly on sale in every sweet shop.

Kids receive dire warnings about talking to strangers. Then, during December, they're encouraged to sit on the knee of a portly man with a red suit, a false beard and halitosis who, almost by definition, is unemployable for the rest of the year. And why do parents wait until they go shopping in order to to smack their kids? 'I'll give you something to bawl about,' they yell at their inconsolable offspring, when it's pretty obvious the kids have something to bawl about already. Yes, it all goes to show that parents are the very people who shouldn't be allowed to have children.

Kids from the suburbs are cosetted: driven to school every morning, and driven home again every afternoon. Then they're kept indoors, because danger lurks outside. But children are at less risk from the bogey-men that haunt their parents' nightmares than they are from the parents themselves. Sad, but true.

Litterdale, in contrast, is a grand place to bring up kids. There's space to kick a football around, without fear of breaking a window. If they want to set up their cricket stumps on the village green, there's no officious park-keeper to chase them away. Whenever they want a bike-ride, there are miles of green lanes to explore. Instead of being confined to a rusty swing in some back-yard, the youngsters of Litterdale have access to what is, effectively, the biggest back garden that any kid could want.

Children need a safe and secure home-life, of course they do, but they need adventure too. And not just the mind-numbing violence of the latest computer games. So it gladdens the heart to see a posse of kids heading off on their bikes, with a rucksack full of sandwiches and bottles of pop. It takes me straight back to my own childhood in Litterdale, when the summers stretched out luxuriantly, like an endless red carpet.

For a year or two I was quite happy grubbing about in the garden: getting dirty, seeing what worms tasted like. Regular kid stuff, but tame. My first attempt at running away from home, for example, was stymied by not being allowed to cross the road on my own. Life became more adventurous once I'd joined a gang. Living in a small Peakland village, we took our inspiration from Enid Blyton's Famous Five rather than the street gangs of the Lower East Side of Los Angeles. So we comprised a particularly unfearsome bunch of desperados. But what we lacked in weaponry, we made up for in resourcefulness.

We built dens in the woods: artless clumps of brushwood to the casual observer, but impregnable fortresses to us. We were prepared, at any moment, to be attacked by wholly imaginary foes: difficult adversaries to defend against. We rooted out crime, even where there was none, and investigated all kinds of suspicious happenings. We found a car parked up in a remote lane, with its windows steamed up. We heard screams, but that was only *after* we'd peered in. We found a man digging in the woods. Assuming, naturally enough, that he was burying a body in a shallow grave, we shadowed his every move. The alternative scenario – that he was just collecting bags of leaf-mould for his garden – seemed far-fetched.

Our gang became quorate, in a strict Enid Blyton sense, by the addition of Kim, a playful Labrador. Though enthusiastic, she didn't seem to understand the role we had earmarked for her, which was to initiate all kinds of new adventures. As loyal fans of *Lassie* and *Rin Tin Tin* on TV, we knew just how much fun a dog could be. So whenever Kim wagged her tail we were ready to say those immortal words: 'Look, I think Kim's trying to tell us something. She seems to want us to follow her down to the old barn.'

Ignoring what she really wanted – a tummy-rub, or a tin of butcher's tripe, we would all troop after her. Not to buried treasure, alas. Not to the scene of some unspeakable crime which we, and not some bungling policemen, would have managed to solve. Not to the old quarry where we might have saved from certain death some hapless rambler who was hanging by his fingertips from the edge of a a precipice. No, Kim would generally lead us to a dead sheep, quietly putrefying in the corner of a field. 'Good dog,' we'd say, not wanting to hurt her feelings, but not thinking too clearly either. Which taught Kim one thing only: that we wanted her to find more dead sheep. Ah, yes, happy days.

✴

AUTUMN

With summer coming to an end, the Litterdale Show is here again. It may seem strange that something as old-fashioned as a village show has managed to survive into the twenty-first century. But it has, and that's something to be grateful for. We're not averse to change; we just like to handle it at our own pace, little by little. No sudden upheavals, if you please. So in the main tent we can still admire the displays of fruit, vegetables and home-made produce. The competition categories remain reassuringly traditional; so it's 'three English apples', 'six broad beans' and 'pot of home-made lemon curd' rather than 'three mobile phones' or 'six website portals'.

The children of Litterdale still exhibit woven samplers, and examples of their neatest handwriting. Their models are made, in best *Blue Peter* style, out of toilet rolls, washing-up bottles and sticky-back plastic. We still have the 'guess the weight of the cake' competition, though this year it nearly had to be cancelled when a goat ate the cake. It took a sudden and triumphant leap of imagination to change the name of the competition to 'guess the weight of the goat'.

When we see the marquees going up in Potter's Field, we feel a sense of community and continuity that stretches back as far as anyone can remember. Yes, to rub shoulders with the crowds on show day is to reaffirm some of the fundamental values of village life. And a wander around Litterdale Show offers intriguing hints about the way that country life is heading.

Many people find their way to Fred's stall by smell alone. His roast pork sandwiches are world famous. World famous around Litterdale, anyway. But this year he's giving concerned carnivores a chance to salve their consciences, by offering 'conservation grade' meat. His customers will feel better, apparently, knowing that the animals they eat have enjoyed meaningful lives.

Each 'conservation grade' cut of meat carries a label, giving a brief history of each pig's life, pet-name (if any) and those endearing characteristics that had marked it out from the common herd. The 'conservation grade' charter promises that the animal will never have been spoken to in a gruff or threatening manner, and will have enjoyed a close physical relationship with the partner of its choice.

The end, when it came, is vouchsafed to have been both quick and painless: a lethal injection administered to the soothing strain of Mantovani strings. Deceased animals are given a short, non-denominational funeral service, before ending up on Fred's barbecue spit. It's a good idea, of course it is. But has anyone polled Fred's pigs about what they might want? Option a: enjoy a long, happy life and die of old age. Or option b: end up in a hot roast pork and stuffing sandwich on show day. Just a thought...

Livestock of a rather more animated kind is paraded around the show ring. The farmers may take a professional interest in the proceedings; for the rest of us, however, one sheep looks very much like another. And this year, bizarrely, it seems we've been proved right. The judges have decided not to award any rosettes at all for sheep, on the basis that most of the entrants appear to have been cloned. We're not too impressed with cloning, if truth be told. Let's face facts: if the scientists were really so clever, they'd be busy cloning animals that fetch rather better prices at auction. Or thoroughbred race-horses. We don't need any more sheep; in the current economic climate the farmers can hardly give them away.

Stalls that used to sell undemonstrative walking clothes – scratchy socks, corduroy trousers and anoraks made of old-fashioned water-absorbent fabrics – are going upmarket. Smooth-talking salesmen are persuading people who never walk in anything heavier than a light drizzle to fork out £200 for a cagoule that not merely keeps torrential rain out but 'breathes' too. For that sort of money I'd want a jacket that could do more than breathe; I'd want it to talk and perform card tricks too. But that's just me.

One stall is devoted to the contentious delights of rural pursuits: 'field sports' to those who follow the hounds, 'blood sports' to those who take a more sanguine view. You can buy picturesque place-mats – featuring hunt sabateurs being hounded over hill and dale – and sign the petition. *'We, the undersigned, wish to maintain our traditional right to hunt foxes. If these animals weren't hunted, the delicate ecological balance would be upset. We are conservationists. We love foxes. And the way we express our love for these fascinating animals is by hunting them down and killing them.'* My own opinion, for what it's worth, is that we should stop hunting foxes and start hunting football hooligans instead. Imagine, two social problems solved at one stroke.

The farmers are taking a more than casual interest in a stall selling perfumes their wives keep wanting for Christmas, but are just too expensive in the shops. They now realise, from bitter experience, that a set of matching saucepans, even ones with floral patterns, do not constitute a proper Christmas present. All the famous names are here, at prices that seem too good to be true. Calvin Klone, now that sounds familiar. 'The perfect gift', as the stallholder points out, with the predictable caveat: 'It's almost authentic.'

The high street banks like to make an appearance on show day if only to remind villagers what a high street bank actually looks like. But memories fade; did banks always have a wheel at each corner? The next generation of Litterdale folk will grow up thinking that banks are like Fred's roast pork stall: only open for business on show day. We'll be back to stuffing money under the mattress. We're all going to be banking on the internet, apparently. But online banking just isn't an option for the more Luddite residents of Litterdale, who are still unsure how to programme a video recorder.

For years the country was the holy grail for over-stressed city dwellers. As they gazed out of their airless offices, over streets choked with cars and robotic commuters, they dreamed of a simpler life, an escape from the rat race. A cottage with roses round the door. Maypole dancing on the green. Warm beer. Village cricket. Rosy-cheeked yokels, in touch with nature and the seasons. All the things that John Major once rhapsodised about. As the paperwork piled up, many an office drone was pacified by this sort of bucolic reverie.

As fantasies went, they were harmless enough, like the thought of sharing a Jacuzzi with the new girl from accounts. And as long as they remained fantasies, all was well. But every now and again some frustrated pen-pusher would make it over the razor wire and, with family in tow, relocate to a place like Litterdale. Typically, it would take just a few weeks to realise the magnitude of their mistake. Life in Litterdale can be rich and rewarding, it's true, but only for people with realistic expectations. Those who know the country only from the pages of glossy magazines are heading for disappointment.

Here in Litterdale we've seen these families come, and we've seen them go. Their fantasies having burst like soap bubbles, they put their houses up for sale, take a loss on their investment, and scurry back to the city. They are left with traumatic memories and a handful of bitter tales with which to enliven their dinner parties. 'Country life?' they'll say, with a shudder of remembrance. 'It was a nightmare.'

Occasionally, the incomers are made of sterner stuff. Violet springs to mind. Having taken early retirement, she decided to move to Litterdale and shake us up a bit. Having been the headmistress of a posh girls' school, she was accustomed to getting her own way. Worse, Violet addressed everyone in Litterdale as though they too were naughty schoolgirls. When a large woman with a braying voice ordered us to 'Tuck your shirt in', or 'Stop slouching', the memories of our own schooldays, however distant, came flooding back. In a manner that would make Ivan Pavlov smile in recognition, we jumped to attention, instantly.

Impervious to criticism, and unassailed by doubt, Violet devoted her retirement years to the thankless task of saving us from ourselves, by pointing out our many shortcomings. At a time of life when many people would be glad to slow down a bit, she seemed to be blessed, or cursed, with boundless energy. Having given our village a long, hard look, she decided we could all do a great deal better. Aspects of everyday life in Litterdale that hadn't changed for generations came under her harsh scrutiny.

To our knowledge, no-one had ever complained about the church bells before. In truth, they sound more percussive than melodic since the bell-tower was struck by lightning, but they do their job of rounding up the faithful on the day of rest. In recent years, with congregations declining, the bells reminded forgetful cooks to put the joint in the oven. Now that most people don't go to church – or sit down to Sunday lunch, for that matter – the bells remain as an inoffensive anachronism. You get used to them; after a few years you hardly notice them at all. Yet Violet was moved to pen a letter to the *Litterdale Times*. She complained that the bells brought on her migraine and suggested, in the strongest possible terms, that they be silenced.

Grateful that he didn't have to write all the letters himself, Scoop printed her missive in full – which only encouraged her to vent her spleen on a regular basis. From Violet's pen came a steady stream of purple prose, griping about the way we live in Litterdale.

Despite her house being called, tellingly, The Old Schoolhouse, Violet grumbled about the lack of amenities in the village. The irony was entirely lost on her. She complained that Litterdale's local shops were closing, even though she only ever went in for a newspaper and the occasional carton of milk. She would drive twenty miles to an out-of-town hypermarket, for her weekly shop, and twenty miles back. The few pounds she saved on her grocery bill were spent instead on petrol. And then she'd moan about being held up by a herd of udder-heavy cows, as they dawdled along narrow roads on their way to the milking parlour. The lack of public transport in rural areas irked her, even though she would never dream of catching a bus herself.

Once she'd pointed an accusing finger at our local farmers, we knew we were heading for a showdown. What got Violet's goat was the mess they made. Piles of muck all over the place. Old tractors abandoned to rain, rust and brambles. Dry stone walls repaired artlessly with rubble. Violet wanted the farmers to tidy up after themselves, so that the countryside resembled more closely the suburbia with which she was more familiar. She didn't like the way the countryside smelled, either, and accused her neighbours of dumping loads of sinus-clearing slurry upwind of her new conservatory.

The farmers of Litterdale don't like being told what to do at the best of times. And these most certainly are not the best of times. It's bad enough when some gormless official, armed with a clipboard, a GCSE in sociology and a sense of his own importance, starts sniffing around the farmyard. But being chastised by an uppity incomer was the last straw. Farmers may be slow to show their emotions, but once roused to anger they can work up quite a head of steam.

No-one knows exactly what happened next. Or, if they do, they're not telling. All we know for certain is that Violet was too traumatised to put pen to paper ever again. We tried to reassure her that *everyone's* house gets fire-bombed from time to time. But maybe we didn't sound convincing enough.

It's November, the month when the members of the Litterdale and District Natural History Society traditionally hold their annual general meeting. Essentially a rather staid occasion, the proceedings are sometimes enlivened by a slide show about dung beetles, or the presentation of a paper about the flora of Derbyshire's railway sidings.

The officials are re-elected routinely on a show of hands; being on the committee of the society is generally regarded as a job for life. The secretary reads the minutes of the last meeting. If, through error or a sense of mischief, he were to read the minutes of, say, the AGM of 1950, it's unlikely that anyone would notice. The treasurer presents accounts that, like Mr Micawber's oft-quoted advice to David Copperfield, are a model of fiscal probity. No treasurer has ever decamped with the contents of the society's bank account, to start a new life in Buenos Aires. In short, an AGM holds few surprises; there's nothing to keep the more elderly members awake beyond the first few items on the agenda.

But there's an air of urgency surrounding this year's AGM. Despite being in existence for more than a century, and having survived two world wars, the society is in crisis. Important decisions need to be taken, decisions that will affect all the members. But will enough of them turn out on a Monday evening in November to make a quorum? This is the society's problem, in a nutshell. It's ironic that apathy may succeed where the Luftwaffe's bombs failed. Having brought the plight of so many endangered species to our attention, the society itself is now in danger of extinction.

Yes, the Litterdale and District Natural History Society has reached this landmark year in a poor state of health. The members are dying off in such numbers that the monthly meetings are more like wakes. And the youngsters just aren't interested in keeping the tradition going. Spending evenings in a dusty room, surrounded by badly-stuffed animals, listening to some Charles Darwin look-alike droning on about the sex life of the water flea, is not a big attraction, frankly, to anyone under retirement age.

There are plenty of young people interested in the environment, of course, but they tend to find bigger, more exciting causes to espouse. Dolphins caught in trawlermen's nets. Ancient woodlands bulldozed to make more accursed motorways. The ozone layer now so full of holes, apparently, that it resembles a threadbare cardigan. And who can resist those sad-eyed Pandas, as they chew their bamboo shoots and tug at the strings of our hearts and purses? No wonder the young folk find it more exciting to dig tunnels, build tree-houses and unfurl protest banners, than to mount a lacklustre campaign to save Litterdale's last clump of some rare lichen.

It's hard to enthuse about endangered species we'd never even heard of until Death beckoned them, with his long, bony finger, towards the eternity of extinction. You can't miss what you never knew you had. I'm sorry, but it's true. For any animal that, like the Dodo, has the twin misfortune to be both rare and unattractive, the future looks bleak indeed.

With so many environmental crises around the world, it's easy to overlook what's happening on our own doorsteps. There's a bittersweet moment, every autumn, when we realise it will be six months before we see another swallow, or hear again the whitethroat's scratchy summer song. But that's all it is, a moment. We confidently expect the summer visitors to return next April. The first swallow to arrive in Litterdale, after its long flight north, is a sight that never fails to lift the spirits. It happens every year, bang on schedule; we don't lie awake at nights worrying about it.

Here in Litterdale we've tended to take our common birds for granted. But the truth is that a lot of our common birds aren't quite as common as they used to be. They haven't disappeared overnight, of course. It's been a gradual process – so gradual, in fact, that we hardly noticed it was happening.

It's easy to rhapsodise about how much better things were a generation ago. With the aid of rose-coloured glass, we reminisce about what we fondly imagine were more contented times. The summers were warmer, children showed respect for their elders and the fields were full of birds. That last memory, at least, is undeniably true. No-one needed to point out the lapwings that performed their aerobatics in the fields, like demented black and white butterflies.

They were everywhere you looked. No-one made a fuss about the skylarks that provided the melodic soundtrack to our summer months. You could find them whenever you wanted.

Spotted flycatchers performed somersaults, in search of their insect food. Yellowhammers sang from the tops of hedges, their plumage the colour of butter toffee. Linnets and redpolls twittered prettily in the trees like free-range canaries. Song thrushes smashed snail shells on their anvil stones; a neat trick, but hardly worth stopping to watch when you could see them do the same thing tomorrow.

Year by year, the picture has changed. Now you can walk out into the fields around Litterdale and not see a lapwing at all. And if you do see one, it's something worth mentioning when you get back home. Whenever you hear a song thrush singing now, you stop and listen, idly wondering when you last heard that first, fine, careless rapture.

It's not a disaster. Not yet, anyway. But it's a wake-up call to challenge our complacency. If we continue to destroy the birds' habitat by grubbing up hedgerows and cutting down copses, the wildlife will dwindle. It's a problem that needs to be addressed, before our songbirds go the way of the dinosaurs at the Litterdale and District Natural History Society.

WINTER

The hills are closing in around Litterdale, as the year comes to an end and winter begins to take our little valley in its icy grip. And what a funny old year it's been, a year with three naughts in it. We won't see its like, not for another thousand years, anyhow. By now, though, the novelty has worn off, like the gilt on all the cricketing trophies the village XI has failed again to win this year. Millennium year may have started with a bang, but now we can barely muster a whimper.

We can see, in hindsight, that the millennium was something that only made sense in anticipation. The moment the clock ticked over from New Year's Eve into New Year's Day, the event was effectively over. Once the fireworks had lit up the sky, and the hangovers had subsided, the other 364 days of the year were always likely to be a bit of a letdown. We've all had fun knocking the Millennium Dome, of course, and we've seen that wobbly Millennium Bridge hastily rebranded as a white-knuckle ride. But the celebrations left us with an empty feeling. As so often happens when we get into party mood, we seem to have spent an awful lot of money without having a great deal to show for it.

Even the Millennium Green initiative failed to fire our imaginations. Litterdale has had a village green for generations, but our local councillors didn't want to pass up all the lovely lottery lolly that was sluicing around. So our lottery grant was spent, instead, on erecting a plastic fence around the village green, and a smart new sign that says 'No dogs'. There was no money left in the pot, alas, to teach the dogs to read, which means that villagers still have to watch where they put their feet. The local dogs don't care about the lottery, or prohibitive signs, or our millennium. Since they live seven years to our one, the canine population probably celebrated their millennium while Roman foot-soldiers were plodding around rural Derbyshire, wondering what they'd done wrong to get such a dreary posting.

Millennium madness has achieved the seemingly impossible, making us all look forward to Christmas. The shops are full of festive fare (as they have been since late October). The newsagent's window is a patchwork of little notices, as villagers try to make some pin-money from unwanted belongings by appealing, perhaps optimistically, to the festive spirit. 'Transmission for 1979 Ford Capri: ideal Christmas present'. 'Two tons of dressed paving stones: ideal Christmas present'. Inside, there's a new selection of Christmas cards, their wording designed to reflect our ambivalent attitude to the festivities: 'Though I'm appalled by the tawdry commercialism of Christmas, I would nevertheless like to wish you the compliments of the season'.

Our vicar, too, is in two minds about Christmas. His church will be full, for the midnight Christmas service at least, and he offers up a little prayer of thanks for that. But he won't recognise most of the people who gaze up at the pulpit, their faces flushed with Christmas fervour, or alcohol, or guilt at not having been to church since this time last year. At least he understands the cathartic effect the midnight service can have on even the most self-regarding of his flock.

Whole families walk arm-in-arm, coats buttoned up against the cold, through streets bedecked with fairy lights, to the warm and welcoming sanctuary of our little greystone church. Up way past their bedtime, the children are wide-eyed with wonder; even their parents feel the magic. The unaccustomed surroundings, the flickering candlelight, the deep shadows, the beautiful carols; yes, even in these secular times the primitive power of Christian faith and fellowship still casts a spell. For the good folk of Litterdale, the midnight service acts as a timely jolt to the system, a potent antidote against cynicism and world-weariness.

By the church door is a traditional nativity scene, assembled by the school-children: a heartwarming tableau of familiar figures that tells the Christmas story. The Virgin Mary watches tenderly over baby Jesus in his wooden crib. Joseph is protective, paternal, yet a bit dumbfounded by events he doesn't yet understand. The three kings form an orderly queue, bearing their gifts of gold, frankincense and myrrh. The entourage is completed by donkeys, gazing over their stall, and what looks suspiciously like a My Little Pony.

Men are notoriously bad at Christmas shopping, leaving it till the very last minute. Christmas Eve is no time to start thinking about what to buy for our loved ones. Once Litterdale's shops have closed up for the holiday, the only place that will stay open over Christmas is the 24-hour petrol station on the by-pass. Which is why there are children in Litterdale who'll wake up on Christmas morning to find their stockings stuffed with furry dice, tubs of Swarfega and five-litre cans of high-performance engine oil. Yes, Christmas is the time of year when we try to be a little better than we usually think we are. But the odds are stacked against us.

Most men would rather have a boil lanced than be dragged kicking and screaming around the shops. And they can't always be left at home, alone, with all those bottles of cream sherry lying temptingly around the place. So this year we have a bold new initiative, to stop them becoming bored and fractious. For the days running up to Christmas, Litterdale's village hall is being turned into a crèche for men. Here, in a safe and supervised play area, surrounded by girly magazines, socket sets and a selection of power tools, men can safely be left for an hour or two while their partners get on with the shopping. If it stops some of those family tiffs over the festive season, we can make it an annual fixture.

The weather is a staple of casual conversation in Litterdale. This isn't town, where people pass on the street without a word or a nod. In a village, with everyone knowing each other, a chance meeting demands a response. But we still don't have all day to stand around and gossip. So what's needed is a simple, formulaic exchange that allows us to inquire briefly about one another's welfare, and then move on.

So the reply to the question 'How are things?' is 'Fine, thanks', or 'Mustn't grumble', or 'This cold snap's playing havoc with my arthritis'. The question is rhetorical; the shorter the answer, the better. There's no need for a long list of seasonal ailments. So a glaringly obvious remark about the weather is a better way to achieve conversational closure.

But, my, how things have changed. Just when we thought we'd got Mother Nature under control, like a dog walking to heel, she starts fighting back. And not just with a nip on the ankle, either; we're getting a comprehensive savaging. From the vantage point of a small Peakland village, we watch, with a mixture of awe and astonishment, as our weather takes an apocalyptic turn.

We used to tune into the weather forecast if we were planning a day out, and the farmers would pay particular attention at hay time. But the weather never dominated our lives in the way it does today. Now we huddle round the radio, like folk used to do in the war, to hear news from the front. We listen intently to the forecasts, even though a lot of them seem like guesswork. After all, isn't 'A 50% chance of rain' just a fancy way of saying 'We haven't the foggiest'? We get no answer to the question that's on everyone's lips: do we need to take an umbrella?

The prophets of doom talk about climate change. Here in rural Derbyshire we were surprised to have a climate at all; we thought we just had weather. But even the experts can't agree about what the future holds. A few years back, after a spate of especially cold winters, the climatologists insisted we were heading towards another Ice Age. That chilly prognosis has been conveniently forgotten; now it's global warming that's all the rage.

Maybe the experts have got it right this time, and Derbyshire will one day enjoy a Mediterranean-type climate. We'll all take a siesta after lunch, and vineyards will blanket the landscape where sheep once grazed. We'll be able to drink a toast to a balmier future with a glass or two of Chateau Litterdale. Or maybe not. After all, the weather round here doesn't seem to be getting milder; it's going to hell in a handbasket.

We used to have rain; now we have storms. We used to have wind; now, bizarrely, we have twisters and tornadoes. We used to have dry spells; now we have droughts that empty reservoirs and transform green lawns into tawny tundra. If there's a pattern to our weather, then we haven't detected it. All bets are off. Anything can happen now. Anytime. It's bewildering.

Over the years, the weather has been kind to Old Ted. Long retired, he props up the bar at the Swan, regaling our more gullible visitors with tall tales of weird weather phenomena culled from memory, his overactive imagination and the pages of *Old Moore's Almanac*. He remembers a traveller who, lost during a particularly savage blizzard one night, hitched his horse to a post. Next morning, when the the snow had melted, he found his horse hanging from the church steeple. Incredible... Whirlwinds would regularly pick up chicken coops, barns – even houses – and deposit them in some other village, miles away from Litterdale, without a scratch. Amazing... If the visitors offer to buy Ted a drink ('I'll have a pint of the strong stuff. And a whisky chaser. And one of those panatella cigars. Cheers'), where's the harm in that?

Now, though, we get weird weather all the time, and Ted's stories don't draw the crowds like they once did. Visitors steal his thunder with experiences of their own: 'What a coincidence. The very same thing happened to us. Just half an hour ago.' Ted now cuts a forlorn figure, harassing visitors with irrelevant observations. If he says 'Aren't these fine buttocks for an old man?' one more time, the landlord will have him barred.

The River Litter used to go about its business with a minimum of fuss. This unassuming little watercourse meandered through the village and flowed beneath the twin arches of the old packhorse bridge, before making unhurried progress down to the sea. It was so familiar that, as long as it behaved itself, we hardly noticed it all all.

Now, though, our river is on the boil. We've been getting as much rain in a single day as we'd normally expect in a fortnight, with water issuing, like some Biblical miracle, from pipes and culverts and holes in stone walls. The swollen river surged intemperately past the bridge, the water the colour of stewed tea. With the fields waterlogged, and the rain incessant, there was nowhere for all that water to go. Something had to give.

When the River Litter finally burst its banks, the floodwater took the line of least resistance, straight through Ted's house while he slept, blissfully unaware, upstairs. He was traumatised on coming down next morning to find muddy brown furniture floating around his sitting room. Looking on the bright side, it's the first time that the soft furnishings in Riverside Cottage have been colour-coordinated. But Ted saw red when his Council Tax went up on the basis that he now had an indoor pool. Where, pray, is the justice in that?

Here we are, in the heart of a Litterdale winter. Memories of last summer faded long ago, and the prospect of summer 2001 seems achingly distant. The recent floods have left everyone feeling a bit twitchy. Those of us who waded disconsolately through their homes, knee-deep in muddy water, will never look at rain in quite the same way again.

We used to enjoy the percussion of raindrops on the outhouse roof. It was vaguely comforting, especially when we were snug and warm inside our little cottages. But not any more. Now it sounds like the beating of war drums, as the Zulus laid siege to Rourkes Drift. It's disturbing.

We used to pull the curtains every evening, and bolt our doors, secure in the knowledge that we'd locked out most of life's unpleasantness. We could sleep soundly in our beds, untroubled by thoughts of intruders. That's the point of living in a village, isn't it? It certainly isn't the nightlife. But, as we've discovered, there's not a lot we can do to keep floodwater out. The sandbags may look business-like, but they're pretty ineffectual, like the pills that Dr Harris hands out to the most persistent malingerers who fill up his waiting room. Yes, an Englishman's home is supposed to be his castle, but right now it feels as though we're living in the moat.

Whenever the village darkens beneath an armada of storm-clouds, and the River Litter threatens once again to burst its banks, a little group of cagoule-clad villagers convenes in silence on the old packhorse bridge. They glare balefully down into the swollen river – it looks like Brown Windsor soup on the boil – hoping to bring down the water level by will-power alone.

What have we done to deserve all this rain? Have we made the gods angry? If so, what will the next affliction be? Well, if Bob the postman is anything to go by, it could be a plague of boils. This isn't something he's keen to talk about, even to Dr Harris. *Especially* to Dr Harris. But there's a lot of legwork involved in a rural round. After delivering letters to everyone in the village, and all the outlying farms as well, all Bob wants is to sit down, put his feet up and read the *Litterdale Times*. For the last few days, though, even this simple pleasure has been denied him.

Left to his own devices, Bob would probably just suffer in silence. That's a man's attitude to illness in a nutshell: if you ignore it, maybe it will go away of its own accord. It's the same attitude that Bob has adopted with all the vehicles he's ever owned, which is why he's never managed to sell any car for more than half what he paid for it. Due to his parsimonious use of engine oil (always a false economy, as Cath keeps reminding him), Bob didn't make a penny when he got rid of his last motor. Worse, he had to pay the guy from the breaker's yard in town to tow it away.

Once Cath had found out what was troubling Bob, by a process akin to reading braille, she packed him off to see the doctor. Bob went, with a show of reluctance. He knew that Cath was right (as she keeps reminding him) but felt obliged to put up a fight for the sake of appearances. His immediate fears were unfounded, thankfully, the waiting room being so full that he had to stand.

At this time of year there are plenty of people in Litterdale who are happy to spend quality time in a friendly, germ-laden environment. Old biddies, mostly. What's the point in cranking the central heating up at home, when the doctor's waiting room is so warm and welcoming? There are dog-eared magazines to read, full of recipes and knitting patterns. There's a tank full of goldfish, more entertaining than the daytime TV they'd be watching if they were at home. Apart from *Countdown*, of course, and that nice Richard Whiteley. There used to be a machine that dispensed hot coffee until Dr Harris twigged why he was dealing with an outbreak of scalded lips and fingers. Yes, if these hypochondriacs aren't ill when they arrive at the surgery, they've usually managed to pick up a sniffle, or better, by the time they leave.

Dr Harris can only spare about five minutes per patient, before writing a prescription for some harmless, sugar-coated placebo. But the other patients have no such constraints upon their time, and are happy to sit around, discussing their ailments and recommending home-grown remedies. Who would have guessed that a hot-water bottle filled with Lemsip could have such a pleasantly analgesic effect?

This is what a lot of doctors seem to have forgotten. Older people want someone to listen to them, to take their problems seriously. They want a doctor who will lean back in his swivel chair, press his fingertips together and give his undivided attention to an elderly lady whose main complaint (apart from her aching joints) is that her children and grandchildren don't come to see her as often as they should. They say that time is a great healer. And a few minutes of a doctor's time, plus a little uncritical empathy, often do more good than a handful of pills. After taking a cocktail of tranquillisers, some of his patients can forget their own names.

And what happened to Bob? Well, Dr Harris gave him a tube of ointment, and an inflatable cushion that looked like an outsized doughnut. He'll have to apply the ointment himself (as Cath keeps reminding him), but the prognosis looks good. In a couple of weeks he'll be as right as... well, as right as rain.

SPRING

When he moved to Litterdale, Mark fulfilled two lifetime ambitions at once. He was able to give up his hated desk job and swap town for country. He found the pace of village life to his liking. Through his conservatory window he could watch mallard ducks sail past; slowly in summer when the river was placid, faster in winter when it was swollen with melt-water from the hills.

Emboldened by banking his severance pay, Mark took over the lease on an empty shop in the village. He lined the walls with shelves, from floor to ceiling, and filled them with second-hand books. The name of the shop almost chose itself: BookMark.

He credited his mother with fostering his love of books. 'Read, Mark, and inwardly digest,' she had said, ambiguously, as he sat on her lap all those years ago. Throughout his childhood Mark took her words to heart. When his friends were outside, kicking a football around, he would have his head in a book.

A few years later those same lads would be down at the disco, having rendered themselves irresistible to the opposite sex by drenching themselves with that great smell of Brut. Mark seldom joined them; unless he'd had a couple of beers he was far too shy to dance. And by the time he'd summoned up enough Dutch courage to brave the dance-floor, he'd generally lost what little coordination he possessed. Instead of being a white-suited John Travolta in *Saturday Night Fever*, Mark looked like a man with ants in his pants trying to send a message in semaphore.

Having read more lyric poetry than was good for a growing lad, he harboured unrealistic expectations about love and romance. While his peers were releasing toxic levels of testosterone, Mark would sublimate his restless libido by taking long walks in the countryside. He wandered lonely as a cloud o'er hill and dale. Overly influenced by Pre-Raphaelite paintings, he nurtured the vain hope of surprising a young maiden bathing in the dappled sunlight of a woodland pool. It never happened, of course. If he did surprise anyone, it was more likely to be a courting couple in a car or someone dumping builders' rubble in a much-loved beauty spot.

Real life failed, predictably, to live up to what Mark read in his beloved books. It was no contest; books never let him down like people did.

Many years later, Mark heralded his entry into the retail trade with a muted fanfair. He concocted a press release in rhyming couplets: a novel approach which failed to impress the editor of the *Litterdale Times*, who buried the news item between the obituary column and the court reports. Nevertheless, the opening party at BookMark was well attended; it's not every day that Litterdale folk get to sup cheap white wine and eat warm sausage rolls at someone else's expense. Everyone went away with a complimentary bookmark and a pleasantly light-headed feeling. One or two people even bought a book.

That initial euphoria was short-lived, however, and the shop would never be as busy again. It bothered Mark at first. Some days he would hardly see a soul, and the amount in the till at the end of the day would largely depend on how big a float he'd put in that morning. He'd buttonhole his customers with tales of how poor business was proving to be, though this willingness to stand and chat was arguably one of the reasons why BookMark was, after all the bills had been paid, barely breaking even.

Mark responded to this retailing crisis in the only way he knew how, by ignoring it altogether. He redoubled his efforts to read his way out of trouble. Lost in a book, he would be startled out of his reverie whenever customers walked in. After a while he came to regard them as unwelcome intrusions. They reminded him of his shortcomings as a bookseller. His body language betrayed these feelings; what had once been a welcoming smile was now a glare. He had a ready answer to those who wondered why he read books all day. How could he recommend titles to his customers if he hadn't first read them himself?

Most people weren't actually customers at all. If the weather was bad, they'd come in out of the rain, stand next to Mark's two-bar electric fire and feign interest in whichever book was closest to hand. Other folk treated the place like a public library. They'd browse for an hour or more, then ask Mark for some book he obviously wouldn't have in stock. Feigning disappointment when he said he hadn't, they would sidle out of the door.

Trade is particularly bad at this time of year. The locals are still ploughing through the books they were bought for Christmas, and visitors don't start to appear in numbers until the Easter bank holiday.

As Mark's accountant reminds him every year, with a sigh, there isn't really enough local trade to keep a bookshop in business. Not in a place the size of Litterdale. And anyone casting a coldly objective eye over the accounts would say the same. The figures just don't add up. To make even a meagre living, Mark has to keep his little shop open till late in the evening. The lights are still burning brightly hours after the other shops have closed up for the day.

Mark loses track of time. Sometimes his head nods lower and lower, until it comes to rest against a pillow of yellowed pages. And, this being March, he dreams of golden daffodils. Hosts and hosts of them, waving in the breeze.

Gardening used to be a congenial way for people to occupy their declining years. If their doctor had told them to avoid over-excitement, they could potter around the herbaceous borders, with a trug over one arm, pruning branches and pulling up weeds. It was a cheap hobby too. There was no need to rifle the petty cash tin for anything more exotic than a new dibber or a packet of lawn seed.

But those days are gone. Gardening is the flavour of the month these days, especially when that month happens to be April. We've all seen those programmes on TV in which an unassuming, but perfectly servicable, back-yard is given an elaborate makeover. The rusting bikes and old mattresses are thrown out, a JCB moves in and two dozen labourers roll up their sleeves. The result: a brand-new garden that will make the neighbours purse their lips with envy.

A short stroll around the village in the pale sunshine of a spring day reveals that, under the influence of TV, Litterdale folk have been splashing out. Mandy, the village's self-appointed seer and sage, has designed her garden using tried and tested Feng Shui principles. Noting, cryptically, that 'Less is more', she's gone for the minimalist approach. She has created what she calls a zen garden; it consists of half a dozen rocks artfully positioned in carefully raked gravel. To Mandy it represents a life of spiritual simplicity. To everyone else, alas, it looks unnervingly like a huge cat-litter tray.

An accountant by trade, Frank is a landscape photographer by inclination. So it's appropriate that he's busy developing his garden. 'It'll look a picture when I've finished,' he enthuses, optimistically, as he takes another trip down to the garden centre. He returns with his trailer piled high with decking: what we used to know, more prosaically, as 'wood'. It's thanks to people like Frank that the man who owns the garden centre is making plans to sell the place, take early retirement and move to the Bahamas.

Scoop used to be known as the Jersey Royal of couch potatoes. Once he got settled on the sofa, after a hard day's work on the paper, only an earthquake would shift him. Or maybe the rustle of a crisp packet. Never known for his gardening prowess, Scoop adopted a simple scorched-earth policy to tackle any weed that had the temerity to show its face between the crazy paving. A flame-thrower was the only gardening tool he owned; it was the only one he needed.

It was watching Alan Titchmarsh and Charlie Dimmock desport themselves on TV that gave Scoop a taste for gracious outdoor living. Barbecues, waterfalls, brick paving, raised beds, wattle screens, trellises, summer houses, pergolas; he quickly embraced the whole ludicrous lexicon of instant gardening.

Scoop's a man who knows a thing or two about deadlines. He has no time for old-fashioned ideas like putting seeds in the ground and watching them grow. He wants a new garden and he wants it *now*. Having watched the gardening programmes, Scoop knows how long it takes to create the kind of garden you see in the Sunday supplements. It takes half an hour.

Violet, our local busy-body, treats her garden like she treats everything and everybody else in Litterdale. As an ex-headmistress, she's used to getting her own way. The lines on her lawn are as straight as the creases in a sailor's trousers. If she tells her lupins to stop slouching and stand up straight, that's exactly what they'll do. Weeds don't stand a chance in her garden. Violet has no need of a flame-thrower; she just has to gives the weeds a withering look.

Despite being flooded out over the winter, Old Ted has decided to go with the flow this year, and create a water feature in his cottage garden. This is in marked contrast to Bob the postman who, thanks to a leaky roof, already has a water feature making slow but inexorable progress down his back bedroom wall. The sound of water bubbling cheerfully over pebbles is supposed to make us feel relaxed and at peace with the world. Yet the same noise, when heard indoors on a rainy night, has the same effect on a terrified householder as listening to termites having lunch.

Bob is convinced that his garden is against him too. He stands at the back door, hurling abuse at his blameless garden plants. 'I've had it up to here with gardening,' he shouts, 'you're on your own now.'

He's vowed never again to lift a spade, or dig up another weed. That's until wife Cath tells him to. Their garden is becoming a sublime profusion. To Bob it's a self-sufficient ecosystem; to his neighbours it's a constant source of irritation.

'What are weeds anyway?' Bob asks, rhetorically, before providing the answer himself. 'They're just plants growing where people don't want them. The best way to get rid of them is just to reclassify them as flowers. I'm hoping for a good crop of dandelions this years. And if I do I'll make some wine.'

Bill, our tourism officer, lives next to the village green. It's one of the prettiest cottages in Litterdale; there are even roses round the door. The garden will provide colourful displays of native flowers throughout spring and summer. Of traditional design, Bill's garden has taken years of hard slog to bring it to this peak of floral perfection. That's hard slog, if you please, not just another trip to the garden centre with a credit card and a shopping list of pointless frippery. Bill knows the truth: when it comes to creating a cottage garden, there's no short cut. Gardening is not a destination, as the TV tosh seems to suggest, it's a journey.

We hardly know what to think of farmers these days. Their standing in the community rises and falls like an overheated stock market. But Les's place in the affections of Litterdale folk is not something that causes him too many sleepless nights. If he thought life was a popularity contest, he'd try harder to remember that there hasn't actually been a spittoon in the tap-room of the Fox since 1974. These days he's got too many other things on his mind. Les farms a hundred unproductive acres up on Heartbreak Hill, you see, and was quietly going broke even before foot and mouth swept across the country like one of the plagues of old Egypt.

Hill farmers are an endangered species. In twenty years' time we'll we wondering not why hill farming declined so quickly, but how come it lasted so long. 'Things just can't get any worse,' Les was saying this time last year, as sheep prices plummeted to the point where it wasn't worth the price of the petrol to take them to auction. But things can *always* get worse, as Les and the other farmers around Litterdale now understand only too well. As the old saying goes: when one door closes, another one slams in your face.

Les is a throwback to another age. He wears a suit – albeit a scruffy one, the kind that scarecrows wear – come rain or shine, and a hat pulled down tight over his ears. He lives alone. There never seemed to be enough time to get around to marriage. In any case, he only ever had one chat-up line: 'Would you like to come back to my place and do a little light dusting?' Predictably, most young women of marriageable age came to the conclusion that, no, they probably wouldn't.

To visit his resolutely grubby farmhouse is like going back fifty years. In fact it's almost exactly like going back fifty years; the headline on the yellowed newspaper that doubles as a table-cloth suggests that time has stood still since coronation year. Left to his own devices, Les has minimised his household chores. What's the point of washing up, he reasons; you're only going to have to do it all over again next month. There's a silvery bloom of dust over everything, but there comes a time when, as long as you don't disturb it by carelessly flicking a duster round, it doesn't get any thicker.

His day begins early. Les puts the TV on while he slurps his tea from a chipped mug. The farming programmes used to be worthy but dull: livestock prices, the weather forecast and maybe a film about what to wear when dipping sheep. But those days are gone, and the news from the country now seems like a never-ending catalogue of disasters. This may account for the unexpected appeal of 'You've Been Farmed', a cheap and cheerful montage of video clips. Red-faced farmers are laughing themselves silly at these amusing and possibly unrehearsed vignettes of country life. Accidents with hay balers, children falling into middens, and cross-species sexual encounters hilariously interrupted by a disgruntled farmhand with a camcorder. Les laughs too, but these days it's a laughter that's tinged with hysteria.

His working day ends late. He responds to every new farming crisis by working longer and harder. But if a man can't make a half decent living by working ten hours a day, is he really going to turn things around by working *twelve*? It doesn't really make any sense, but farming is in his blood. He doesn't know anything else. Everyone seems to have an opinion these days about what farmers should be doing. Convert a barn into a guest house, run a petting zoo, sell premium foods over the internet. But Les wouldn't know a website from a hole in the ground. And overnight guests would soon regret not booking into somewhere more salubrious… like the Bates Motel.

He is, in every sense, the last of the line. At one time he regretted not having a son to take over the farm. But not any more. If Les, with years of experience behind him, can't make ends meet, what chance would a greenhorn have?

It seems almost inconceivable that the countryside is changing so dramatically. But, in truth, it's always changed. A hundred and fifty years ago, many voices were raised in protest when the Peakland landscape was enclosed with dry stone walls. Now we would be equally strident in their defence if we heard they were to be knocked down. When the railway came to the Peak, those same voices complained about the viaducts being built to span the steep-sided dales. Now we're slapping preservation orders on them.

Les will carry on farming until he himself is planted in good Peakland earth. After that, who knows? What will become of his ramshackle farmhouse, up on Heartbreak Hill? Dale Head Farm could be transformed into a handsome holiday home for a commodities broker from Sheffield. With a few additions of no architectural merit it could be the clubhouse of yet another golf course. If it stays a farm, I'll eat my hat. If it stays a farm and turns a profit, I'll eat Les's hat too!

SUMMER

The holiday season is well underway. More visitors are coming to Litterdale than we had any right to expect just a few short weeks ago. Thank goodness. The summer won't be a total write-off after all, though everyone who has a teashop or a guest house will be happy just to get through the rest of the year and still have a business to run.

The landlord of the Fox used to treat visitors like vermin, during the summer months at least. And if any of them took umbrage, they were welcome to take their custom elsewhere. He wasn't bothered; there were always plenty more tourists around to fleece. But this summer is different, and one side-effect of the foot and mouth epidemic has been to make everyone a little more courteous to the visitors who *do* come. There is an unaccustomed air of civility in Litterdale's alehouse; it makes the locals nervous.

The downside is that visitors think it's a buyers' market. Just because the village is going through a bit of a bad patch, some of them are treating Litterdale like a Moroccan souk. The landlord of the Fox is doing his best to be agreeable, but the next customer who tries to haggle over the price of a pint and a packet of pork scratchings will find himself spreadeagled in the road, with a boot-print on his arse.

The Litterdale and District Agricultural Show is the summer's major casualty. It's the first time since the Second World War that the tents won't be going up on Potter's Field. Bill, our tourism officer, had to bite the bullet and make some difficult decisions. With so many events being cancelled, he opted to pulp thousands of glossy tourism brochures. In their place is a hastily concocted list of alternative attractions and diversions that will hopefully serve the dual purpose of opening the visitors' wallets, while keeping them well away from farms, footpaths and livestock. To pad out the schedules, even the most mundane events are listed: car-boot sales, blood donor sessions, a visit from a peripatetic chiropodist. Difficult times require desperate remedies.

Bill has been as even-handed as possible in his recommendations. He mentions the Swan, for example, as the best place to enjoy a leisurely lunch. Even the Fox gets an abbreviated mention, along with some much-needed advice: 'On no account speak to the locals unless spoken to, and never, ever complain about the beer.'

A craft fayre each weekend is proving quite a draw, though God knows why. The word 'fayre' should be warning enough. But as soon as they arrive in Litterdale, the visitors seem to leave their critical faculties in the pay & display car-park, along with their family saloons. Why else would they part with folding money for most of the tat on sale in the village hall? Log cabins made from lollipop sticks. Hand-made cards. Wishy-washy watercolours of well-loved Peakland landmarks.

Let's be straight on the matter. Most crafts are hobbies – excellent therapy, no doubt, for idle hands and troubled souls – but not businesses. These crafts-people ought to be told, 'think twice before putting your deformed offerings on sale, and, if they're log cabins made from lollipop sticks, don't even bother to think once.'

With so many paths and green lanes still out of bounds, Bill has created a set of self-guided walks that stick resolutely to Tarmac. Starting, sensibly enough, from the car-park, the Litterdale Trail visits most of the village's landmarks. The village green (the 'Keep off the

Grass' sign has been mothballed till things get back to normal). The duckpond ('It attracts many species of ducks. Mallards mostly'). The cricket pitch ('The scene of many epic performances. Mostly by the opposition'). The office of the *Litterdale Times* (interesting, no doubt, to those who want to watch a large man in a swivel chair eating cake). The River Litter (you can see how far the floodwaters rose during the winter; the high water mark extended well above the knee of Old Ted's gardening trousers, which he hasn't got round to washing yet).

There's one group of visitors that needs no invitation from the likes of Bill. And here they are, enjoying the ambience of a warm summer Sunday. The village green is transformed into an impromptu display of classic motor-bikes. And, a few yards away, lounging on the benches outside the Fox, is an impromptu display of classic motor-bikers. Yes, lock up your daughters, the Hell's Angels are here...

To hear some of the villagers talk, in hushed whispers, you'd think we'd been invaded by aliens. The bikers' reputation goes before them. But that's all it is, a reputation. Respectable parents shield their children's eyes as they walk past, which merely lends the bikers an unwarranted air of mystery and menace. But these superannuated outlaws are, in truth, about as menacing as a troupe of boy scouts. There's no need to lock up your daughters. Maybe just keep granny indoors.

These guys may try to look fierce, but they're not looking for a fight any more. It's too risky at their age; some of their blood groups have been discontinued. They're at that difficult time of life: too old to cut up their own food, yet still too young to be Radio 2 disc jockeys. They loll around on a summer's day, squinting into the sun, and talking about, well, bikes mostly. Good British bikes that sound like an artillery barrage, and drip oil all over the road. None of your Japanese rubbish.

And when the day is done they'll gun those bikes all the way home, through narrow Peakland lanes. They'll make a few old ladies jump. Then it'll be mugs of Horlicks, a few shortbread biscuits and an early night. Yes, their hell-raising days are over, they're the Mild Bunch.

It's high summer in Litterdale. The election provided us with some harmless entertainment, though there's a limit to the excitement that can be generated by a one-horse race. Since there was no space on the ballot paper to vote for 'Democracy', 'Fascist Junta', 'Banana Republic' or 'Enlightened Dictatorship', the only choice was between one load of identikit politicians and another. Or, for those who were bored with politics altogether, there was always the Green Party.

Down here in rural Derbyshire, we're used to straight talking. Some of those politicians may reckon to be big shots up in London, but that doesn't give them the right to swan around Litterdale as though they owned the place. Especially since we won't be seeing any of them for another four years. They'll promise the earth, if that's what it takes to win our votes, but you'll find they've got their fingers crossed behind their backs. We're impressed by deeds, not words. We'll listen, with one hand cupped around an ear, to whatever a politician has to say, but we'll make sure to keep the other hand on our wallet.

Once the polling booths were dismantled, and the ballots counted, village folk were in general agreement: whoever you voted for, it's the Government that got in. The only thing that's changed is that this lot don't have the luxury that all new administrations have, to blame everything on the last lot. We could have voted for the Natural Law Party (with the obvious fiscal advantages of yogic flying) without the even tenor of village life being greatly upset. Even if it was a little green man from the Planet Zob waving from the steps of Number Ten, the cows would still need milking twice a day. And considering the state of our bus service, yogic flying sounds a rather more convenient way of getting around.

It's true that most people in the village own cars. But that just makes life increasingly difficult for those that don't. Yes, once we've sold our soul to the infernal combustion engine, it's the devil of a job to get it back. The bus company reacts to every plea for a better service by cancelling yet another bus. There isn't much point asking anyone when the next bus is due; even the woman on the telephone helpline can offer nothing more than a hollow laugh.

Mandy, the village's seer and sage, owns one of those half-timbered Morris Travellers. It looks like Anne Hathaway's Cottage on wheels. She parks it all around the village, the exact location dependent on sound Feng Shui principles. It's always there when she gets back; only a short-sighted thief of unsound mind would think to try the door handle.

Mandy claims all kinds of special insights, based on the interpretation of signs, portents and premonitions. Of genuine powers there appears to be more hint than evidence; just a meaningful tap on the nose here, a knowing smile there. If you press her on the matter, and wonder what she really can foresee, she'll say, with that little smile and one raised eyebrow: 'Well, I knew you were going to say *that*.'

Her faith in intangible forces extends to her car. It's knackered, basically. When the second-hand car salesman in town saw her coming, he rubbed his hand together; he knew his monthly sales bonus was in the bag. He, too, has special insights; he can spot a soft touch a mile away. Mandy's body language, her aura if you will, seemed to be suggesting: 'I've had my frontal lobes removed and I've got a Barclaycard.'

There was a Morris badge on the back of the car, but a Toyota badge on the front. There's just no pride in the spot-welding craft these days. The salesman told Mandy it was a special edition, but because she wanted it so much, she could have it at the same low, low price as the regular model. That was the clincher.

It's the ideal car for people who, like Mandy, don't really approve of cars. Since she voted for the Green Party at the election, she'd like to do without a car at all. But, as she points out, how else can she take all her empties to the bottle bank? The flaw in this argument seems to have passed her by.

Everybody's car breaks down occasionally, but Mandy's is the only one in the village that actually breaks down in tears. The trouble is that she doesn't know why it goes, and she doesn't know why it stops. It seems to run on the motive power of pleas and prayers. Instead of filling up with petrol she tries, through the power of thought alone, to persuade the needle on the petrol gauge to creep out of the red. It means she misses a lot of appointments, sometimes by a matter of days.

Whenever the car splutters to a halt – a regular occurrence – she knows exactly what to do. She opens the bonnet and gives the engine a long hard stare, hoping to shame it back to life. If that doesn't work, she resorts to desperate measures and cleans out the ash-trays. That represents the limit of her mechanical knowledge; the next step is to ring a mechanic or (if the problem's with the bodywork) a carpenter. Everybody else in Litterdale is keeping their fingers crossed, hoping the car will hold together long enough for her to drive it to the breaker's yard.

✸

There's a regular bus service from Litterdale into town. That, at least, is the impression you get if you stand at the bus-stop and read the timetable. There's no need to hurry; whatever time you arrive, you'll have ages to wait before a bus comes. There are children in Litterdale who have managed to reach school age without encountering one. 'What's that big red thing, dad?' 'It's a bus, lad. Take a good long look; it may be the last one you see round here.'

The Litterdale route, though scenic, does not feature strongly in the bus company's strategy for the future. By reducing the number of buses to a bare minimum, and running them at inconvenient times, the company hopes to prove the route is uneconomic. Then they can do what they've wanted to do for years: shut it down altogether and drive yet another nail into the coffin of rural transport.

An integrated transport system is a mythical sort of beast, like the phoenix, the roc and the unicorn: something we've all heard about, but few of us have seen. Okay, we can catch a bus into town, do some shopping, and catch a bus back home to Litterdale. We'd just like to be able to do it in a single day.

A week on the Litterdale run is viewed, by the bus drivers, as a punishment. But if they want to get their regular routes back, they'll have to follow the bus driver's manual to the letter. This requires them to accelerate as fast as possible from every stop, then braking equally hard at the next one, thus making the journey as uncomfortable as possible for their passengers. With a glance in the mirror and a well-timed tap-dancing routine on the gas pedal and the brake, they can transfer an old lady and her shopping trolley from one end of the bus to the other in less time than it takes to say 'Hold tight at the back'. It's moments like these that make the bus driver's life worthwhile.

There's a lot of information that the bus timetable fails to mention. Such as how long your journey might take. Don't be lulled into any false sense of security by the idea that the bus is just going into town. Imagine your're going on an African safari, and pack accordingly. At the very least, you should take some provisions for the outward trip. If you're attacked by crazed pensioners, suffering from hunger and acute tannin deprivation, you may be able to appease them with some cheese and pickle sandwiches and a flask of weak tea. It's August, remember, so wear a scarf or cravat as a face mask; it will help to keep out the dust and the flies and the suffocating smell of lavendar water.

Some of the bus drivers have such a poor sense of direction that they have to stop periodically and ask the passengers which way to go. And it's not unknown for the drivers to organise a whip-round to fill the tank up, when they've run out of petrol. By the time the bus rolls into Litterdale once again, having covered half the county, most of the passengers will be delirious. No wonder the Litterdale run has been re-classified as a white-knuckle ride.

Bus useage is a sure indicator of social standing, winnowing the wheat from the chaff. Those of us who go by bus generally have no other option. Without a car, we're at the mercy of those mendacious bus timetables. Those of us who don't travel by bus would rather undergo abdominal surgery with a rusty machete than be forced to wait around at the bus stop by the village pond. Petrol would have to to be £100 a litre before we'd give up the sheer convenience of sitting in a traffic jam with hundreds of other stationary cars, drumming impatient fingers on the leatherette dashboard.

A pity, really. It can be quite fun to bounce around the country lanes in a bus, at least for those blessed with strong constitutions. But we look at buses in much the same way as our great-grandparents looked at the workhouse: in fear and dread that one day we too might be reduced to this final humiliation. Yes, if a businessman with a briefcase were to get on a bus, he might just as well wear a badge on his lapel that read 'I've got the sack, they've taken my company car back and I'm on my way to the Job Club. Kill me now; it would be a blessing.'

The social niceties of bus travel don't end there. Do you sit next to someone you've been chatting to in the bus queue? To do so might seem a little forward, while not to do so might be seen as stand-offish. You're sitting next to someone on a crowded bus which almost empties at one stop. Should you now move to a new seat, and risk offending your neighbour, or stay where you are? We need a manual of our own, 'Debrett's Guide to Bus Etiquette' perhaps, to help us mind our manners.

Last week, a bus was involved in a minor accident in Litterdale. A jaywalking duck was the culprit, apparently, though the duck's opinions on the matter were not sought. The driver was on his way back to the depot, so his bus was empty, thank goodness. By the time the police had arrived, though, the bus was packed with groaning pensioners. Who, in all honesty, can point the finger of recrimination at our senior citizens for spotting such a heaven-sent opportunity? After all, it's not every day they get the chance to leap aboard a bus, feign injury and put in a claim for compensation. If the ruse works, maybe they'll be able to afford a little runabout, and not be forced to queue for buses any more.

*

AUTUMN

A lot of visitors think our village takes its name from all the rubbish they leave behind. They're not aware that the source is actually the River Litter, one of Derbyshire's less celebrated watercourses. Their confusion is understandable; by this time of year, after another busy summer, Litterdale is looking a bit of a tip.

The water in the duck pond is almost hidden beneath a floating raft of crisp packets and empty cans – through which the ducks make laboured progress. The lightest breeze sends paper and cartons skittering along the cobbles; the take-away tumbleweed of a throw-away society. The war memorial is crowned incongruously with a traffic cone. The rubbish bins are overflowing with the unwanted souvenirs of a day out in Litterdale. Encouraged by this squalor, and too idle to drive to the council rubbish tip, someone has tipped a lorry-load of rubble in the lay-by.

After a prolonged dry spell, the river is as low as anyone can remember. The water has a grey, lifeless look. It doesn't really flow; it oozes. With a sharp knife, you could cut it into slices. If you see a fish jump, it's probably just trying to catch its breath. The only thing our fishermen are likely to catch is impetigo. You wouldn't throw a match in; the river might just go up in flames. Yes, as summer is coming to an end, the River Litter is not looking (or smelling) its best.

A condensed history of the last century could be read from the artefacts that are turning up in the mud and the silt. By searching immediately down-river from the old packhorse bridge, the kids are turning up old stone ginger beer crocks, and those old glass bottles with the marbles in the neck. Throughout the ages, men have stood on bridges, bottle in hand, wondering why life has dealt them such unplayable cards. Having finished the beer that has been the cause of this morose introspection (and not, as they had imagined, the cure), men have taken a small satisfaction in hurling the bottle into the river, before staggering back home to their beds.

The Litter is giving up its other secrets too: rusty old bikes and bedsteads, milk-crates and mattresses. A wonky-wheeled supermarket trolley is wedged in the mud, even though the nearest supermarket is more than ten miles away. One mystery, at least, has been solved. It's many years now since Bob the postman decided to extend his repertoire of skills beyond cracking his knuckles and wiggling his ears. He could have taken up Scrabble or marquetry; it was just a shame that he went into town and bought a trombone instead.

Every day, after he'd finished his rural round, Bob would pucker up and practise his scales. Sometimes he'd even make a stab at producing a recognisable tune. Unfortunately, Bob has Van Gogh's ear for music, and his discordant expeditions into the hinterlands of modern music shattered many a peaceful afternoon. Litterdale is a small village and Bob's caterwauling seemed to permeate every home. Even double glazing offered little respite from his atonal tootlings. Yet no-one seemed able to find a tactful way of telling Bob to put the proverbial sock in it. Nobody wanted to upset the man who delivered the mail.

One day the trombone was there in the closet where Bob kept it. The next day it had gone. Bob searched the house from top to bottom. It was nowhere to be seen, of course. Polite enquiries around the village were met with a wall of silence. There were many people under suspicion, music lovers mostly. Bob thought his trombone was lost for ever… until last week, when he saw something gold glinting in the pale September sunshine as he carried the last of his letters across the bridge. He retrieved the instrument with a stick, and put it in his mailbag.

Bob was amazed that his trombone had turned up after all these years. Bob's wife, Cath, was amazed too; she thought she'd long since seen the last of the accursed thing. 'You know,' he said, flexing the mud-caked slide, 'with a bit of work it could be as good as new.' It wasn't until later, when he was idly watching *Crimewatch* on TV, that Bob wondered who had stolen the trombone in the first place. 'Maybe there'll still be some fingerprints on it. I could let the police have a look.' 'I don't think so,' said Cath. 'While you were watching TV I gave it a quick rub-down with a damp cloth. I'm sorry.'

Seeing our river in such a state has shamed us all into action. How can we scold the kids for tossing their sweetie wrappers on the pavement, when the evidence of more adult indiscretion is here for all to see? Showing a unity of purpose not seen in the village since the war – when pots, pans and park railings were dispatched, to be melted down and made into Spitfires – we had a big clean-up at the weekend. Able-bodied villagers congregated at the bridge after lunch on Sunday, dressed for salvaging duties – which ranged from wellies, fishermen's waders and kids in their swimming trunks and costumes.

Over a long, hot afternoon we hauled that rubbish out. It was sobering to see just how much junk there was; we filled a rubbish skip right up to the brim. Let's hope that people will have a little more pride in the village, and think twice before using the river so thoughtlessly.

To thank everyone for their efforts, the landlord at the Fox put on a barbeque. Bob was going to use the occasion to announce that his trombone had miraculously turned up again. Maybe play a few tunes. 'Best not,' said Cath, 'everyone's had such a good day. Why spoil it?'

Here in Litterdale there's a distinct nip in the air. The nights are beginning to draw in. The horse-chestnut tree on the village green has yielded up a bumper crop of conkers. Despite the competing attractions of TV and computer games, it's somehow reassuring that the village kids still compete against each other with conkers threaded on strings.

They stand on the green, hurling sticks into the upper branches. The conkers they can't reach always look bigger and better than the ones that are lying on the ground. The kids pounce on the spiky shells, opening them up with impatient fingers to reveal the smooth, silky, lustrous perfection of the fruit within. The gloss soon fades, of course, giving our children a valuable lesson about disappointment and loss and good things not lasting for ever, a lesson which their adult lives will probably confirm.

This venerable old tree has stood here for centuries. If only it could talk. Imagine all the events it must have witnessed over the years. How many relationships have blossomed beneath its spreading branches; how many people have relaxed in its shade? Mind you, if the tree *did* start to talk, it would probably just mean I'd neglected to take my medication again.

This is a busy time for Norman, Litterdale's resident handyman; almost as busy as spring, summer and winter, in fact. When something around the village needs doing, Norman doesn't wait for someone else to spring into action. He knows, from past experience, that he could be waiting till Doomsday. So once October is here Norman can be found on the village green, raking the fallen leaves into a big pile to burn. When pungent smoke is rising from wet leaves, with Norman in close attendance, we are left in no doubt: Autumn has rolled round once again.

Norman's an adaptable sort of fellow; he could turn his hand to just about anything. But the same can't be said for the hill-farmers of Litterdale. They work all hours, in all weathers. They're persistent, even bloody-minded. They respond to everyday crises phlegmatically. They know all there is to know about sheep and dairy cattle and how to patch up a broken-down wall. The trouble is that they're so busy working that they seldom have time to think about the future of farming. On the rare occasions that they do, it fills them with a nameless dread. So there's every incentive just to carry on as they are and let tomorrow take care of itself.

Hill farmers are being told, in no uncertain terms, to be more imaginitive. This may be feasible for some of the younger folk, but it's not so easy for an old stick-in-the-mud like Les. Any kind of change is anathema to Les, whether it's a penny on a pint in the pub, or some new bureaucratic inanity designed to make farming even more difficult today than it was yesterday. But he's never been one to turn easy money down. So when a bloke from Bakewell waved a wad of notes under his nose, in the tap-room of the Fox, Les was in the mood to listen. It seemed like a good deal: some tax-free beer money just for the use of one of his fields for a day. That's why signs went up all around Litterdale, directing Sunday morning traffic into a car boot sale.

Les had heard about car boot sales, though he'd never quite understood why car boots – rather than spare tires, say, or wing-mirrors – should be the focus of so much attention. When he wandered down into his bottom field, to see what all the fuss was about, he was gobsmacked to find it transformed into a Moroccan bazaar. Displayed artlessly on makeshift stalls was just the kind of junk that was lying around his own unlovely home: chipped coronation mugs, dodgy videos, old biscuit tins, novelty ashtrays, rusty tools, that elusive third LP by Bucks Fizz and Polaroid cameras for which they stopped making films in 1974. The only difference was that all this junk had price tags.

There was even a stall selling home-made chutneys and conserves. This was yet another surprise for Les, who'd assumed that 'money for jam' was nothing more than a colourful turn of phrase. He wandered around the stalls, shaking his head. He'd long suspected that the world was going mad, and here was solid proof.

It wasn't so long ago that people went to church on a Sunday morning. They looked to the man in the pulpit for guidance and reassurance. But the habit's been broken, and it will take more than gimmicks like Hymn Number Bingo to bring the congregations back to fill the empty pews. Nevertheless, they find there's a big hole in their lives where blind, unquestioning faith used to be. So they go car-booting instead, to rummage through other people's cast-offs and maybe pick up a bargain. This is a kind of faith too, as the money-lenders no doubt said to Jesus before he chased them out of the temple.

Here, in the bargain basement of budget retailing, there's plenty of stuff to keep the browsers busy. 'Antiques of tomorrow', as the stallholders say: what used to be described, more prosaically, as 'rubbish'. Those who have suffered the misfortune of having their car radio stolen may find a replacement on one of the stalls. They may even find the one that was taken in the first place. This is half the attraction of car boot sales: an opportunity for boringly law-abiding citizens to become Arthur Daly for a few hours, and to rediscover the lost art of haggling over stolen goods.

A sign on an elderly Hoover reads 'Genuine reason for sale'. The stallholder tries to reassure a punter that it's in good working order. 'I'll be here next week,' he lies, 'if you have any trouble with it.' ('It's a genuine reason for sale, all right,' the stallholder whispers conspiratorially to Les, in passing. 'It's knackered.')

It's that time of year again, when Litterdale folk get together to watch the fireworks. Yes, the annual general meeting of the Litterdale and District Pool League, now in progress in the back bar of the Fox, can be a combustible affair. It should be just a matter of minutes to rubber-stamp a simple agenda, but something happens to even the most taciturn participants whenever they preface a sentence with the words 'Mr Chairman'. It brings out the bar-room lawyer in all of them; they become pedantic and argumentative. No point of order seems too insignificant to warrant a motion, a seconder, maybe a counter-motion, followed, eventually, by a show of hands. Only for someone to find fault with the small print, rephrase the motion in a slightly different way, and go through the whole charade once again.

After a few beers the pool team representatives are giddy with power, even though it's only the power to keep everyone in the Fox up way past their bedtimes, debating points of order that have no meaning beyond these walls (and precious little inside them either). They start dissecting aspects of this simple and diverting pub game that they'd largely taken for granted. Like Rule 34(a), never a contentious directive. Until now.

Notions of sportsmanlike conduct are notoriously difficult to pin down. Players whose parting shot to a victorious opponent is along the lines of 'I'll have you outside, you cheating bastard' are unlikely to be reined in by a minor rule change. But it's eventually agreed, after heated debate, that beating an opponent to death with the butt end of a pool cue is an action that runs contrary to the spirit of the game, and that a penalty of two free shots will be awarded. A second such offence will forfeit the frame. Harsh, perhaps, but fair; we've seen far too much of this kind of thing lately.

Hands are raised, excitedly, to instigate some new motion, and are hurriedly taken down again, as the chairman seeks nominations for the posts of secretary and treasurer. Doing some real work (behind the scenes, throughout the year: a thankless task) doesn't have quite the same appeal as shooting their mouths off at a meeting, so the pool players of Litterdale find this a convenient moment to slope off to the bar.

The start of the indoor games league is a bittersweet occasion. Summer is long gone, and winter stretches out ahead like a long and dreary road. Hibernation seems a very attractive proposition. Who wouldn't settle for curling up under a duvet till spring? Visitor numbers have declined to a trickle, walkers mostly, and we have the village to ourselves once more.

The landlord of the Fox is in conciliatory mood, hoping to attract the locals back through the doors. So out goes the over-priced tourist menu, and in comes good, wholesome, unpretentious fare. Pies, stews, dumplings, chips; maybe a side order of lard or suet. It's comfort food, solid chloresterol to send a man away with a lead weight in his stomach and a light feeling in his head. There's rumoured to be an Egon Ronay inspector buried under the car-park, but don't let the landlord hear you say so.

Games night in the Fox is a convivial affair, giving even the laziest villagers the chance to display their prowess at darts and dominoes, pool and whist. Old Ted, for example, even finds crown green bowling too strenuous. His idea of exercise is to hide the TV channel changer. Yet he turns out for the darts and dominoes team come rain or shine. The only time in recent memory that he missed a games night was during last year's flood. And that was only because he couldn't get the outboard motor started. That's how keen he is.

The fire is banked up, and the ale flows freely. The landlord surveys his grubby little empire with grim satisfaction, as he waves a duster over the scotch eggs. Hygiene is not a high priority at the Fox. A regime of benign neglect gives the place an earthy charm. He listens to the random percussion of dominoes being laid – with knocking noises, like a friendly ghost, whenever a player can't go – and a triumphal flourish as the last tile goes down. Dominoes: our weekly reaffirmation that life could be worse.

Darts, on the other hand, is a more hazardous affair. You wonder who first had the idea of recreating indoors the noble sport of archery. Dispensing with bows, bringing the arrows down to a size that can be gripped between thumb and forefinger and – what imagination! – encouraging the participants to drink beer at the same time. In a sane world, darts players would be isolated in a padded room, where the only people at risk of injury would be each other. Throwing sharpened missiles in a crowded, smoky bar seems like a recipe for disaster. In any other context, the building would soon be surrounded by armed police, shouting terse instructions through loudhailers.

Across the road, the upstairs room at the Swan is transformed. It's amazing what dim lighting and a few Chianti bottles filled with candles can do. Once a month the room becomes the Litterdale Folk

Club, where adenoidal social workers routinely murder ancient songs of lust and revenge. Looking on the bright side, though, it means the pub doesn't actually need to apply for a music licence.

'Hi, I'm Kevin,' says Kevin, 'I'd like to start the evening off with a song about whaling.' He runs the Litterdale Folk Club only because he'd never get a singing spot, on merit, at any other club. When he fluffs verse 12 of his 15-verse ballad, his attempt to start again from the very beginning is drowned out by a desperate rush for the door.

WINTER

Violet is Litterdale's resident busybody, the self-elected expert on just about everything she thinks we ought to know. She's the living proof that dog owners grow to look like their pets. Once she gets her teeth into some new idea, she's just like her little Yorkshire terrier: tenacious, single-minded and impossible to shake off. She was walking her dog one day in autumn, engaging the mutt in animated, though one-sided, conversation. As she passed the old quarry she noticed, to her horror, that someone had thoughtlessly dumped a lorry-load of rubbish into it. What a cheek!

Somebody had to spring into action. As usual, Violet put herself up as the one and only candidate and voted herself into the job. Since then she's been waging a one-woman campaign against the despoilers of our landscape. Yes, Violet's become an eco-warrior. Or maybe that should be eco-*worrier*. She worries about global warming. She worries about acid rain. She worries about the hole in the ozone layer. Most of all, she worries us.

Don't get me wrong; our poor, battered, beleaguered world needs all the help it can get. Those who wantonly despoil it must be made to mend their ways. If God really has given us custody of the planet, then we should be expecting a knock on the door any day now from a team of celestial social workers. Our lame and shame-faced excuses – 'I don't know, maybe the earth slipped and fell, these things happen' – will fool nobody. Look after the planet? Most of us find it hard enough to look after a *goldfish*.

No, what bothers the good folk of Litterdale is being lectured to by an overbearing woman, in the tone of voice normally used to reprimand a naughty child. Perhaps we should be giving Violet a pat on the back for being so concerned, so single-minded and so incontrovertibly right. There's a fine line, though, between doing the right thing and being a complete pain in the neck, and it's a line she oversteps rather too often. She's got something to say about every subject under the sun. And, unlike our depleted stocks of fossil fuels, Violet's opinions seem infinitely sustainable.

She should relax now and again, and maybe let someone else have a turn at carrying the planet. But there's no room for complacency, she insists, while we face the threat of global warming. Low-lying Peakland towns could be lost beneath the flood-water. Litterdale itself could become a coastal resort blessed with a Mediterranean-type climate, where trees laden with citrus fruit would add welcome splashes of colour to the limestone landscape. Problem? What problem?

Violet's ideas are irreproachable, her logic beyond question. And it's pointless to argue with a woman who puts the welfare of the planet at the top of her priorities. If she tells you to don your wellies, wade out into the river and pick up all the old bicycles and bedsteads, the easiest option is just to do it. There's no point suggesting you were were just on your way to the Fox for a leisurely pint. 'Pint? Pint? How can you even *think* about such things at a time like this?' she'll suggest tartly. It's always a time like this, of course. Your pint will have to wait.

But the strain of being ideologically correct – all day, every day, with just an hour off for lunch – is beginning to tell. Her lofty ideals make her susceptible to altitude sickness. And some of her recent stunts, though well-meaning, have backfired badly. When she bought a fur coat for the winter, the saleswoman ensured her it was made of recycled fur. The fur was indeed recycled, it used to be a silver fox. There were red faces all round after that.

Violet has been picketing the local abbatoir, where fat porkers are dispatched on a daily basis to meet their maker. It's humane, of course, to give pigs the opportunity to die with dignity, though Violet's suggestion of leaving a flask of whisky and a pearl-handled revolver in each animal's stall is greeted with snorts of derision by the slaughtermen.

She liberated the trout from the tank in a restaurant, and decanted them into the river. It seemed a good idea at the time; how was Violet supposed to to have known they were *sea*-trout? Being summonsed for polluting the River Litter with dead fish won her no plaudits from the local Friends of the Earth group. They voted her off the committee. Now she's just an associate member, a *Friend* of a Friend of the Earth.

Litterdale's village green looks splendid. Every year about this time, for as long as most of us can remember, Norman has hauled out the boxes of fairy lights from under the stage in the village hall.

He chunters away to himself as he drapes the lights between the branches of the trees. He shouldn't still be doing this. Not on his own. Not at his age. Not with his angina. And definitely not balanced precariously on a rickety step-ladder. Once he's finished, though, villagers come out to admire his handiwork. Norman switches on the lights with a flourish, and gets a small ripple of applause. Those who have marvelled at Blackpool illuminations may find the lights of Litterdale a little short on spectacle. But they give the village a homely air, and this is all we really want.

Our mood is thoughtful, a little sombre. This is a time for quiet reflection, for gathering the family around us. Even those well-heeled villagers who normally spend Christmas abroad – soaking up the sunshine while the rest of us shiver – have decided to stay in Litterdale this year. We've re-ordered our priorities; counting our blessings, not just bemoaning our fates. Even the usual platitudes sound different. Seldom have the words 'Peace on earth and goodwill to men' been said with more conviction.

Les has a traditional view of Christmas. He loathes it. From his familiar soap-box, propping up the bar at the Swan, he bends the ear of anyone who lingers a nano-second too long about the shortcomings of the festive season. Les moans about Christmas from the moment the first tinsel-wrapped stock appears in the shops, all the way through to Twelfth Night when the decorations that haven't already fallen down are taken down. Les is spared this tiresome chore because he never puts any decorations up in the first place. Dale Head Farm is as uncompromisingly spartan at Christmas as it is during the rest of the year.

He moans about the escalating cost of Christmas, even though it's years since he last bought anyone a present. In a good year, his Christmas dinner might consist of a packet of 'Turkey & Stuffing' flavoured crisps, washed down with a few cans of industrial-strength lager. In a bad year he may not bother with the crisps. And the only reason Les doesn't moan during Christmas dinner is because he eats it on his own.

There seemed no reason why this Christmas would break this long-established pattern, so Les was mystified to find himself inundated by invitations. Bob and Cath, moved by pictures of refugees on TV, decided that charity should begin at home. They didn't want to see Les on his own at Christmas. He was welcome to join them for roast turkey and all the trimmings, as long as he promised to keep his boots on. Violet, too, was all affability. Once she had locked away the silverware, she suggested Les might like to pop round, after milking the cows, for a schooner of sherry and a few mince pies. Mandy wondered if Les would like to share a salad and a glass or two of home-made parsnip wine. This latter option held little appeal. 'Salad isn't food,' Les confided to the landlord at the Swan. 'Salad's what food *eats*.'

Disorientated by all this unexpected attention, he accepted a last-minute invitation from Old Ted to bag sileage and heckle the Queen's speech on TV. This, as the pub regulars were surprised to hear on Boxing Day, was the best Christmas that Les could remember.

It's a shame that it takes world conflict to make us all a bit more considerate towards each other. But Steve, our vicar, is not complaining. He never thought he'd live to see what's happening at St Breville's. While there's little of architectural interest about the undistinguished greystone building, it still merits a few lines in the tourist brochure. Mostly for the hand-knitted hassocks, the handiwork of the WI. They feature local landscapes, Biblical scenes and in one case (maybe someone wasn't briefed too well) the grinning face of Micky Mouse. We appreciate that's not enough to entice afficionados of fine old churches. But, hey, if there's another church in Derbyshire dedicated to St Breville, the patron saint of toasted snacks, then we've not heard about it.

Things were different in years gone by. Everyone used to go to church on Sunday morning or, if they didn't, they made sure to have a good excuse at the ready for when the vicar called. So, like a gourmet who loosens his trouser belt notch by notch, the church expanded over four centuries, to keep pace with the ever-increasing population of Litterdale. Sharp-eyed visitors can spot the joins in the masonry where an aisle was widened or a tiny chapel added. The last major building work took place in 1875, the result of a bequest by a wealthy local man who felt the need to atone for some of his sharper business practices. In an unhappy coincidence this was the same year that congregations began the long, slow decline that has continued ever since.

By the time Steve moved into the vicarage, congregations had become embarrassingly small. Scattered worshippers looked lost in the ranks of pews. The thin, reedy voices of Steve's elderly parishioners almost disappeared in all that space, echoing feintly up into the vaulted ceiling.

In a manoeuvre that lovers of parlour games would recognise as musical chairs, Steve took a row of pews out every year and moved those that remained ever closer to the lecturn. The empty spaces were filled with screens, on which children's paintings were displayed. Almost by sleight of hand, Steve created a church within a church, to reflect what the village of Litterdale has become. And now, as he surveys his congregation with quiet satisfaction, he knows his work has paid off. Who would have believed it? For the first time in a long time, and not just for the midnight mass on Christmas Eve, people are coming to church again. In a decade of tending his Litterdale flock, Steve has never known the church so busy.

Perhaps some people feel there's a big empty hole in their lives. A hole that can't be filled by a racy sports car, a new shade of lip-gloss or the short-lived satisfaction of giving their credit card some serious hammer. Perhaps they feel anxious and disorientated, as old certainties don't seem quite so certain any more. Perhaps they've weighed their lives in the balance, and come up short. Whatever. All Steve knows is that if things carry on like this, he'll have to put some of those pews back.

Regular attendance is a steep learning curve for some of the less experienced parishioners. Steve has to explain that, no, the absence of White Christmas in the hymnal is not merely due to a printing error. And the numbers on the hymn board have nothing to do with rollover week on the National Lottery. No matter. As he stands in the pulpit, gazing down at the sea of expectant faces, Steve gives a short and silent prayer of thanks.

Litterdale dozes fitfully through another Peakland winter. We don't get many visitors at this time of year, but look what they're missing. The village green, rimed with frost, sparkles in the pale sunshine. Smoke snakes lazily upwards from cottage chimneys, and hangs in the valley. The cottages that surround the green look ancient, organic and elemental. It's a timeless scene, painted in muted greys and browns. The archetypal English village, as long as you ignore the TV aerials. If Litterdale were made of skin and bone, muscle and sinew, rather than stone and slate, you might say the village was hibernating. You'd have to listen carefully to find a pulse. Of vital signs there are few, on a Sunday morning in February: just a single line of footprints across the frosty grass.

A portly figure is hunched over a tripod, wrapped up warm against the cold that turns his breath into mist. It's Frank, Litterdale's resident photographer, busy twiddling the knobs on his brand new camera. He's wearing the sort of down-filled jacket that makes him look as pneumatic as the Michelin Man. The ear flaps on his hat give him the half-witted look of an elderly Labrador; the fingerless gloves look like hand-me-downs from Fagin.

The camera was a Christmas present to himself. It joins the extensive collection of cameras and lenses that he already owns. Since a lot of those lenses wouldn't fit his new purchase, he went out and bought a new range of lenses too. Wide-angle, telephoto and a monster that looks like an anti-tank bazooka, which could take a characterful head-and-shoulders portrait of an ant at a thousand paces. And, since you shouldn't put new wine into old bottles, Frank splashed out on a smart new camera bag as well. This is what can happen when a man pulls in a good salary but has no family to put a brake on his immoderate spending habits.

Frank doesn't see himself as spendthrift, of course, just enthusiastic. He thinks his enthusiasm is about photography, though it's actually the cameras themselves that get him excited. By the time the credit card bills roll in, there's always some fancy new machine that will take better pictures than the camera he bought last month. He just can't resist the allure of matt-black hardware, that's all.

His pride and joy this month is a Cartax 796, with a power-drive. By keeping his finger on the shutter, he could run through an entire film in twelve seconds. For reasons known only to Frank, he sees this as highly desirable. Yet all he's done since Christmas is to take the camera out of the bag, and run his fingers over those sinuous curves. Today is the first time he's actually put a film in.

The camera boasts a baffling array of buttons and programmes and back-lit displays. It takes him months to get to know the idiosyncracies of a new camera, especially since the instruction manuals are mostly translated from the original Japanese by someone for whom English is not his first language. Thankfully, the 796b will hit the market any day now – with a laser viewfinder, or speech recognition, or some other dubious feature that will make him go weak at the knees with desire.

Frank would be happy to show off the new machine to anyone who happened to be up and about. But the good folk of Litterdale have already peered out of their windows and seen the frost on the ground. And, more to the point, they've seen Frank pootling around on the green. These are two good reasons to stay in, bank up the fire and find some odd jobs to do around the house.

There will be Sunday papers to read, when they finally arrive. The paperboy, Bob and Cath's lad, Ben, used to finish his Sunday paper round by the time most folks in Litterdale were enjoying their first cup of tea of the day. But the papers seem to expand every week, with some new lifestyle supplement, and the poor lad's legs are beginning to buckle under the weight.

If he's not careful, he'll end up with as many vague and undiagnosed ailments as his dad. Bob has committed a long list of symptoms to memory, in case anyone asks how his feeling. Which nobody does. Somebody with a wicked sense of humour bought Bob a medical encyclopaedia for Christmas. By the time he'd read a couple of chapters, Bob identified with all manner of conditions from Beri-Beri to Dutch Elm Disease. The only illness that sounded too far-fetched was the one that everyone agrees he's got: an acute case of hypochondria.

Sunday is a day of rest for a postman, which gives Bob the opportunity to discover a few more symptoms. He stands in front of the bathroom mirror. It's not a pretty sight. He sticks out his tongue, then puts it back again quickly. He gazes at his reflection and sees how he'll look in twenty years' time. His chin is stubbly – but instead of looking rugged and manly, he just looks like old-man Steptoe. Bob feels brittle; one false move and a bone could snap. He's got an irritable bowel, a grumbling appendix, a murmuring heart; yes, even his internal organs are telling him he's not a well man.

And now, to cap it all, he's come down with flu. It's one of those gender-related illnesses (women get colds, men get flu), so he's not getting much sympathy at home. Cath told him to stop moaning, or go and see the doctor. Dr Harris didn't have much time for him either, and told him to take a powder. And when Bob asked the chemist to make something up for him, the chemist said there were fairies at the bottom of his garden. Bob can do without that kind of sarcasm from a man who sells suppositories for a living.

SPRING

I t's March. The more optimistic villagers may be able to convince themselves that Spring is here. Realists, on the other hand, know that Winter still has a few tricks to play.

Rain and meltwater have left the ground saturated. Farmers are walking sodden fields and, in consequence, filling Dr Harris's waiting room with pungent agricultural odours and bad cases of trenchfoot. Les is up on Heartbreak Hill, putting a new sheepdog through its paces. His language is the most colourful aspect of a scene that seems to have been re-tinted from a more limited paint chart, mostly in Pennine Drizzle and Sleet Grey. If the darkest hour is just before dawn, then the gloomiest time of year seems to be just before Spring erupts with new life and colour and birdsong.

Les whistles, waves his stick, and calls the dog by name. But he's frustrated, and the name Les calls the hapless dog isn't the one that's engraved on its collar. So the dog becomes confused, and the sheep scatter in all directions. Les has heard about Dolly the sheep, and wishes all his sheep were cloned. Then they might all run in the same direction. They would all look the same too, but Les wouldn't find this a problem.

Les has an unsentimental view of his animals. There's no point getting too chummy with any beast whose last port of call will be the abattoir. In the Biblical parable the sheep that was lost was worth more than the other ninety nine. That rings a little hollow in the Derbyshire Dales of today, since all sheep, whether lost or found, are worth about the same: bugger all.

Every year, at lambing time, there are always a few sickly lambs that need special attention. Les will hoist them over his shoulder, the very image of the Good Shepherd, and take them back to Dale Head Farm. Though he will sit up half the night, feeding them milk from a baby's bottle, the ones that survive will soon be back in the fields again, fending for themselves.

The new sheepdog will find its place at the farm, but that place is outdoors. Les would no sooner have a dog inside the house than invite a pack of rats to come in and make themselves at home. Working dogs belong in the yard, chained up and lying doggo until a group of unsuspecting ramblers walk through the farmyard. That's the moment the dogs leap out, barking insanely, their chains pulled as taut as a ship's hawser. Let's face it, scaring hikers half to death is one of the few perks of a demanding job.

Two months ago the villagers were singing the same tune: a mournful ballad about the perils of self-indulgence and the urgent need for self-improvement through the rigours of self-denial. Fat, flabby and listless after the big Christmas blow-out, and cash-strapped from rushing round the January sales, they vowed to make changes in their lives. Their new year's resolutions ranged from the pragmatic ('I will never, ever, drink after-shave again') to the hopelessly unrealistic ('I will go jogging every morning').

Everyone relishes an opportunity to be a little bit better than they usually think they are. But hangovers subside, eventually, and it's exhausting just watching those fitness videos. By the time that March comes around, most of these resolutions have been forgotten – consigned to the cupboard under the stairs along with the dumb-bells and the fondue sets.

Bob the postman is bucking the trend. He lit up a slim panatella on New Year's Eve, and declared it would be his last. He wasn't going to cut down; it was 'cold turkey' or nothing. And, amazingly, he hasn't touched the evil weed since then. Cath is supportive, but keeps a watching brief. Bob's not known for the strength of his convictions, so this display of will-power is particularly impressive.

He started smoking at about the age of fifteen, because it seemed to be an integral part of growing up. Like millions of other deluded adolescents, Bob thought that smoking would add a little glamour to his mundane existence. But all he did was to welcome into his life one of the most perniciously addictive drugs known to mankind. His dad had issued dire warnings about the dangers of smoking and drinking. Unfortunately he had a Capstan Full Strength in one hand, as he spoke, and a tumbler of single malt whisky in the other, which rather negated the effect of his fatherly advice. This, too, seemed to be a part of growing up: attaining a level of hypocrisy to match your parents.

Giving up is never easy, and Bob's had a few bad moments. He has to stay away from the pub, where the plumes of cigarette smoke are as beguilingly hypnotic as the swaying of a snake charmer's cobra. At moments of stress he still reaches, automatically, into his jacket pocket for a packet that isn't there. The low point was aiming a kick at the cat, in a display of nicotine-related petulance.

Slowly but surely the cravings are subsiding. From being a twenty-a-day man, he has joined the ranks of smug ex-smokers. And, let's face it, people don't come much smugger than that. Bob embraces abstinence with evangelical fervour, always ready to stop and talk to people about how much better he's feeling. His clothes don't reek of cigarette smoke every morning, and he doesn't wheeze any more as he makes his morning round.

Best of all, as he enthuses to Cath, he can really taste his food now. This is something Cath knows already; for the past two months she's been adding fresh basil to the spaghetti sauce, turmeric to her curries and cloves to the apple pies. It's her secret contribution to Bob's titanic effort in helping to give that cold turkey a bit of spice.

Bill, Litterdale's tourism officer, is feeling rather pleased with himself. And why shouldn't he? A two-day brainstorming session (with Bill and his staff holed up, at the council's expense, in a rather splendid four-star hotel) has produced a host of new visitor initiatives. After so many months of misery, in an area of the country that relies so much on tourism and animal husbandry, it's vital that the rural economy gets a shot in the arm.

The session was a great success, with all local tourism initiatives now coming under one umbrella, 'Tourism 2002'. Everyone agreed that this name was catchy and up-to-date. The icing on the cake (Black Forest gateau, incidentally, and 'rather good') was an exciting new slogan. 'Litterdale, it's probably closer than you think.' Bill rewarded himself with a liqueur coffee for dreaming that up. The other candidate – 'Litterdale, Derbyshire's Best-Kept Secret' – appeared to contain a subliminal criticism of the tourism department, and was voted down, five to four, after second helpings from the sweet trolley. Yes, however much that brainstorming shindig cost, it was money well spent.

Tourism 2002 is exceeding expectations. A record number of tourist brochures have been dispatched, each and every one a triumph of anodyne banality, and bookings are well up on last year. We wait for the visitors to come, our fingers poised over the cash-tills like typists waiting for dictation.

The sign that greeted motorists – 'Litterdale welcomes careful drivers' – was taken down last year. After all, even the most accident-prone drivers have cash to spend, and the pubs, cafés and guest-houses of Litterdale didn't want to miss out on their share. If the National Association of Reckless Drivers (and Affiliated Operatives in the Bus and Taxi Businesses) had wanted to hold their AGM and dinner dance in Litterdale, all we would have said was, 'When and where?' Yes, that's how bad things were round here. Norman, bless him, has put the sign up again, and given it a quick, rust-inhibiting wipe with his oily rag. Everyone hopes that summer will be a belter; some of the businesses around Litterdale couldn't survive two disastrous summers in a row.

There are one or two people in the neighbourhood – no names, no packdrill – who believe their front gardens aren't complete without a burning mattress and a clapped-out car propped up on house-bricks. Bill doesn't share their aesthetic, of course; a tourism officer has to lead the way in keeping Litterdale looking its best. So Bill's cottage garden, overlooking the village green, will bloom in colourful profusion this year, as it does every year.

Spring has finally arrived in Litterdale. People we haven't clapped eyes on since last October are crawling out of the woodwork, pale and blinking after another long winter of sunlight deprivation. If winter is like being hermetically sealed inside a Tupperware container, spring is like an unseen hand prising the lid off.

There are sights to cheer the most jaded souls. Colour is returning to the landscape, like the blush to a maiden's cheek. The grass is greening up. The trees around the old packhorse bridge are laden down with blossom; from a distance it looks like freshly-popped popcorn. The scene is softened, for a few days at least, by these candy-floss colours of spring. It's like being in a particularly sentimental Walt Disney cartoon; you half expect a flock of bluebirds to land on your shoulder and trill in three-part harmony.

The trees are filling with songbirds, their little chests puffed out with springtime fervour. What they are actually singing about is anyone's guess. We like to imagine it's a heartfelt paean of love, from a cock bird to his mate, as she puts the finishing touches to her nest. Or maybe it's something rather more prosaic, like 'This is my tree... piss off'. Who knows for sure?

The spring sunshine penetrates the darkest, cobweb-strewn corners of our homes – revealing what havoc has been wreaked by another winter of household neglect. Squalor shames us into action, leaving us with difficult choices: should we clean the cooker or just move house? We wave feather dusters around, without much enthusiasm, succeeding only in whipping up the dust in thick clouds. Over recent months a deep layer of dust has helped to lag pipes, stop draughts and impart a silvery bloom to the furniture. But now the dust seems to dance in the rays of light. It's Disney dust.

The harsh spring light makes a searching examination of our lives too, with rather more clarity than we either need or want. We feel a strong urge to shake ourselves out of our lethargy. And, with our failings and foibles mercilessly exposed, this is a good opportunity to take stock. New Year is no time to make life-changing resolutions; the time for self-improvement is *now*.

This is the time to get fit, to keep those promises to walk down to the paper shop instead of just taking the car. Pessimists can watch the blossom blowing away in the first stiff breeze. Optimists, on the other hand, can give their boots a coat of dubbin, pack a rucksac with sandwiches and Kendal Mint Cake, take a deep breath of good country air and set out to enjoy a Peakland ramble in the sweet springtime air.

That's what Bill's going to do this weekend. Mind you, he's already planning another departmental get-together; maybe a long weekend just after Christmas, somewhere a little closer to Alton Towers, to dream up another snappy name for the unseemly clamour to claim the tourism pound. 'Tourism 2003' is an early favourite, but let's not be too hasty.

Like swallows but bigger – and with wallets – the visitors are back. With each weekend that passes, the car-park gets busier. Purposeful walkers lace up their boots and, keeping their wallets tightly closed, head for the hills. Others – the moochers, the grockles, the rubbernecks – need a little more entertaining. As long as that's a pub lunch, or shopping for nick-nacks, then we can oblige. Litterdale isn't Disneyland, but we're still happy to take day-trippers for a ride.

What about the visitors who want a bed for the night and a hearty breakfast next morning? Mandy, Littledale's New Age representative, opened her doors to guests a couple of years ago. With mixed success, it must be said. The sign in the front garden of Primrose Cottage promised 'Bed and Breakfast', whetting the appetites of passers-by with such luxuries as 'flush toilets', 'wall-to-wall carpeting' and 'hot and cold running water in every room'. Primrose Cottage had been 'Officially vermin-free since 1999', not a claim that every house in Litterdale could match. Despite these proud boasts, visitors weren't exactly beating a path to Primrose Cottage.

When Mandy bought the place, it was a picturesque ruin. The wind whistled through the cracks in the window frames, like Larry Adler tuning up. She 'cured' the leaky roof by the simple ruse of not venturing into the loft any more, and masked the more malodorous smells with incense. There was a greasy, grey-green Galapagos beneath the bathtub, where plants that shunned light could quietly thrive. She coped with the grime and neglect in the only way she knew how, by using dimmer lightbulbs. By the time she was down to 4-watt bulbs, she was bumping into the furniture.

When it all got too much Mandy would sit cross-legged, wherever she could find an uncluttered area of floor, and resort to a tried and tested mantra. 'I am happy, fulfilled and brimming with self-confidence,' she would drone, morosely. 'I know my own worth and I have well-defined goals. I have much to offer the world, and my well-rounded personality will attract luck, money and love. I see only positive things happening to me in future.'

Primrose Cottage was a loose rung on the property ladder. The only way she would ever be able to sell the place was by dismantling it and auctioning off the bricks as individual lots. In desperation she bought a new self-help book. After a brief perusal of *How to Attract Money into your Life*, she did as the author suggested, and visualised coins of many denominations pouring out of a golden cornucopia and into her cupped hands. The results exceeded the wildest expectations of everyone except Mandy. After a decent interval of six months, a distant cousin died, leaving Mandy a tidy sum in her will. Sceptics may mock such credulity, but the cheque went into Mandy's bank account, not theirs. Perhaps these books really do work, after all.

Mandy adopted a two-pronged strategy for renovating Primrose Cottage. She's a firm believer in Feng Shui, the venerable Chinese art of stating the blatantly obvious. By harnessing these principles to the proven power of ready cash, Mandy hoped to breathe new life into the house.

With the help of a local builder who knew which side his bread was buttered, she put the kitchen where the bathroom was, converted the box-room into an en-suite bathroom, raised the roof by two feet and created three more bedrooms. She had the house sand-blasted but, intriguingly, only on the inside. A plan to move the entire house three feet to the south ('to get the morning sun') was abandoned, but only with the greatest reluctance.

The work is nearly finished. The last item on the agenda is to have the overflowing rubbish skip taken away. An eyesore it may be, but how on earth did we manage before the humble rubbish skip was invented? Belying its humble appearance, a skip is actually a sophisticated recycling system – proving that one man's rubbish is, indeed, another man's treasure. When we hire a skip we are, albeit unwittingly, inviting our neighbours to indulge in a traditional, two-part ritual. It happens all over the country, and it goes like this.

Step one: wait until the attention of the skip-hirer has been momentarily distracted. In the few seconds it takes to tie a shoe-lace, or rummage through a handbag for the car-keys, there is just enough time for doors to open and for neighbours, laden down with unwanted possessions, to tip-toe purposefully towards the skip. When the skip-hirer turns around to look at the skip again, he does a deadpan double-take of the kind that a white-faced Buster Keaton all but patented. The last door is closing, noiselessly, and the skip (*his* skip) is filled to overflowing with other people's detritus.

Step two: this is conducted at a more leisurely pace. Over the next couple of days, the neighbours give the contents of the skip a cursory examination as they walk past, followed, under cover of darkness, by furtive forays to liberate perfectly serviceable stuff that others have so casually thrown away. There's wood to burn. And a chair: a perfectly fine chair that will look as good as new after a lick of paint. And that old radio; it probably only needs fresh batteries. And so it continues. By day three the skip will be almost empty once again, allowing the hirer to fill it with his, or in this case, her own junk. Job's a good 'un...

Even the most sceptical villager is impressed by Mandy's efforts. After all the upheavals Primrose Cottage is looking good. Here's an object lesson in how to transform a sow's ear into the proverbial silk purse. She will be opening her doors to guests any day now. We hope things go well, and that the days of food poisoning and private prosecutions will be nothing more than distant memories.

SUMMER

We spent a small fortune, a couple of years ago, on what we were reliably informed was a solar-powered sundial. It seemed an appropriate way to commemorate the Millennium. It was only when we'd put it into position on the village green that some bright spark said that every sundial is solar powered. Yes, we'd been had. And every time we saw the accursed thing, it just served to remind us how silly we'd been. So we took it down. In any case, why would anyone want to remember the Millennium? It's been and gone. Good riddance, we say.

We should have learned our lesson by now. Nevertheless, a lot of villagers were keen for Litterdale to mark the Queen's Golden Jubilee with something more tangible than a monumental hangover. But with the coffers empty after the sundial shambles, we needed to raise more money. The traditional method, here in Litterdale, is to rattle a collecting tin under the noses of drinkers while they're enjoying a pint in either the Swan or the Fox.

The well-heeled patrons of the Swan will dip their hands in their pockets if a tin is rattled loud and long enough. But it's a strange irony that the rougher the pub, the more money the regulars seem to raise for charity. And few pubs in the Litterdale area are rougher that the Fox. It's the sort of pub where bogus MOT certificates can be had for the price of a pint. And if you win more than 50p on the fruit machine, the biggest problem is getting out alive. But when it comes to charity, you only have to mention children or animals to have big men with broken noses getting dewy-eyed and sentimental.

They'll peel fivers from suspiciously thick wads of notes, eased out of back pockets. They'll erect piles of pennies on the bar. They'll organise all kinds of events – often involving feats of brute strength or dressing up in women's clothing. So when the landlord suggested a duck race, to raise money for the jubilee fund, the idea went down well. Even after the disappointment of learning that no real ducks were involved, the regulars were keen to roll up their sleeves and muck in.

They bought 3000 yellow plastic ducks from a place that sold yellow plastic ducks in bulk; it's amazing what you can find in the *Yellow Pages*. Every duck had a different number painted on its bottom, and visitors and locals alike were encouraged to 'buy' one. Sales were bouyant, thanks to the terrific prizes donated by local businesses. First prize: A luxury weekend, all expenses paid, at Primrose Cottage Guest House. Second prize: A free session with a visiting chiropodist. Third prize: Dinner for two at the Fox (pudding not included). By the time the great day had arrived, all the ducks were spoken for. So far, so good.

The River Litter is a watercourse of many moods: a mere trickle in high summer, a roaring torrent after winter rain. Sometimes it misbehaves – like last year when it sluiced through our homes. But mostly it goes quietly about its business.

On the day of the Duck Race, crowds lined both sides of the river in eager anticipation. A net was stretched taut between the stanchions of the old packhorse bridge, the finishing line, to catch the ducks. Two hundred yards out of town, upstream where the main road crosses the river, a tipper truck full of ducks was backed over the parapet. On an agreed signal, 3000 yellow ducks slid from the back of the truck and hit the water simultaneously.

The event, as a genuine race, was over there and then. The breeze, though light, was still stronger than the river's sluggish current.

Three thousand yellow ducks massed together, like the Zulus at Rourke's Drift. But instead of rushing pell-mell downstream, the ducks closed ranks and sullenly refused to move. When the breeze quickened it merely pushed ducks to the water margins, where they got stuck in the reeds.

After half an hour, a few dozen ducks had floated as far as the weir where, years ago, water was diverted towards the waterwheel of the old mill. But instead of taking the plunge, the ducks floated around in ever-decreasing circles. After an hour of surreal inaction, the crowd began to get restless. Little kids, blessed with the attention spans of particularly inattentive goldfish, were demanding chips and ice cream. People started to throw stones. Stewards waded into the water and tried to hurry the ducks along. Men fell over and got drenched; people laughed; words were exchanged. The ducks remained mockingly uncooperative.

A few ducks eventually arrived at the finishing line, but only because they'd been thrown there. 'It's a fix,' shouted those onlookers who hadn't already drifted away. What a shambles.

The *Litterdale Times* subsequently printed this statement from a Duck Race spokesman, who asked to remain anonymous. 'It is difficult to know what to say about the shameful events of last weekend. We are stunned. The entire duck-racing community is stunned. We have witnessed many sporting disasters in recent times. The abortive Grand National of 1993. Mike Tyson chewing Evander Holyfield's ear off. Derek Pringle. But these are as nothing compared to Saturday's debacle. The river level was unseasonably low, making the going firmer than we (or the ducks) would have liked. Some people in the crowd suggested the ducks weren't trying, though it was probably their boos and catcalls that disorientated the ducks and made them swim around in circles. No-one comes out of this fiasco with much dignity. There will be a steward's enquiry. Heads will roll. Thank you.'

Beneath this terse statement was a display advert: 'Almost 3000 plastic ducks for sale. Nearly new. No sensible offer refused.'

The winning duck, incidentally, was number 475, bought by the landlord of the Fox. He has decided not to take up his prize, but to raffle it at a later date. In the meantime he has decided to take a short holiday, and will not be available for further comment about the Duck Race, or anything else for that matter.

✳

The village is a magnet on sunny weekends; people come from miles around to celebrate the fact that the banks are shut. Two kinds of motorists feel drawn to explore the narrow, twisty lanes around Litterdale. There are those who want to pootle around at a stately 20mph ('Oh look, dear, a cow. And there, if I'm not mistaken, is another one.' 'More tea, dear?' 'I don't mind if I do'), and those who see the Peakland hills as a race-track, their very own Indianapolis 500. The prospect of these motorists sharing the same stretch of road is not one to savour. It's a convincing argument for Litterdale folk to stay home, draw the curtains and watch a re-run of *The Italian Job* on TV. Compared to the mayhem on our country roads, those Mini drivers look like paragons of courtesy.

For some unfathomable reason, Litterdale fills up with the sort of vehicles we only ever see in summer. Ancient VW vans announce their arrival with heart-stopping backfires, palls of diesel smoke and unlikely slogans ('Kathmandu or Bust', 'Just one Careful Owner') painted on the side. They give Litterdale the attractive look of a car-breaker's yard.

Visitors park up their beach buggies, soft-tops and natty little sports cars around the village green, so that everyone has the opportunity to admire them. Having shelled out a small fortune for new, in-car stereo systems, the proud owners naturally want to turn up the volume, crank up the bass, and hear what it sounds like. And where better to conduct this aural experiment than a tranquil Peakland village? As anyone living within five miles of Litterdale is painfully aware, it sounds like a man armed with a leg of lamb trying to break out of an IKEA wardrobe.

Last month's disastrous Duck Race left a lot of people with red faces. Not the ducks themselves, of course, which maintained their air of jaundiced inscrutability throughout the proceedings, and the stewards' enquiry that followed. A lot of people, particularly those whose ducks had failed to finish the course, wanted the winners dope-tested. The race organisers refused, mostly due to a sudden outbreak of common sense. We've moved on, thank goodness, and visitors to Litterdale this summer are enjoying a wide choice of family events.

The Green Weekend has been and gone. It was a great success, by all accounts. Even folk living in rural Derbyshire are glad to be reminded, on a sunny weekend, that the world is going to hell in a handbasket. Shopkeepers and café proprietors appreciated the extra business, even those who'd happily vote for nuclear power and badger baiting.

Local pressure groups had stalls on the green, offering good advice. Why pay exhorbitant heating bills, the crowds were asked, when they could harness the power of the sun? And, yes, solar power might seem to make sense in a place like Litterdale, what with its sunny winters and balmy summers. But the truth is rather different. We've got to face up to the fact, no matter how unpalatable it may be, that solar power is just not as sustainable as these eco-warriors suggest. If you leave your solar powered torch on charge by mistake, the next day will be cloudy and dull. Just coincidence? I don't think so.

Wave power is being touted as the Next Big Thing. Poppycock. If we start sucking the energy out of the waves, the seven oceans of the world will soon be as flat as millponds. It stands to reason. And it's been estimated, by people with too much time on their hands, that the methane produced by cattle would meet most of the world's energy needs. All we need is a way to collect it. Yes, if we listened to these well-meaning folk, the earth would be not only a better place, but flat too.

We were told that the Men of the Trees would make an appearance over the Green Weekend. But they had to cancel (a bad experience with a blackthorn, apparently). Their place was taken by Theresa

Green, 'a well-known arboreal activist' according to her business card. She gave a short, heartfelt address, asking us all to think twice about felling trees. 'Would we cut trees down so blithely if we could hear them screaming?' she asked. Well, we might, if they screamed all night and kept us awake.

Of course, once you advertise a Green Weekend, you tend to attract the lunatic fringe too. A 'Honk if You Love Peace and Quiet' campaign had a mixed reception. And the 'Put the Landfill Site Where the Poor People Live' petition is yet to reap rewards. But give it time.

Let's be straight. 'Looking after the planet for future generations' makes a useful, if meaningless, slogan. But, as Old Ted points out, we'd be more concerned about saving the planet if these self-appointed 'greens' could answer this one simple question: 'What on earth have those future generations ever done for *us*?'

Never mind. It's the height of Summer. Foot and mouth is a distant memory (and let's hope it stays that way). Visitors still come to Litterdale; however much we moan about them, we'd be moaning a whole lot more if they decided to stay away.

✳

Life is a gamble; from the cradle to the grave. Even in a quiet, well-ordered community such as Litterdale, danger stalks the unwary. As Old Ted knows only too well, you can be perched on a bar stool one minute, exchanging pleasantries with the landlord of the Swan, and a moment later you can be choking on a honey roasted peanut that went down the wrong way. An immovable object lodged in the windpipe isn't something you can write to an agony aunt about. It concentrates the mind, wonderfully, like having a pistol pointed at your head. Time is of the essence. Yes, if Dr Harris and his wife hadn't been enjoying an all-you-can-eat Sunday lunch in the carvery, Old Ted might have become just one more statistic in the annals of snack-related injuries.

If you'd asked Ted about the Heimlich Manoeuvre up to that point, he'd have guessed it was a Second World War stratagem aimed at opening up the Russian front. But, red-faced, bug-eyed and gesticulating wildly, he was in no position to argue as the doctor, moving remarkably quickly for a big man, sized up the situation. Dr Harris approached Ted from behind and took him in a huge bear hug; it looked like he was lifting a sack of potatoes. With no time for social niceties, the doctor drove his clenched fists, with irresistible force, into Ted's solar plexus. The peanut was expelled with such velocity that it ricocheted off two walls, before embedding itself harmlessly in a bowl of guacamole. Old Ted was so grateful that he allowed the doctor to buy him a drink.

Life's a gamble all right, though we're not too good at reckoning the odds. We'll happily spend a quid or two on the lottery, even though the odds of winning the jackpot are a distant 14,000,000 to one. 'It could be us,' we tell ourselves, with the optimism of the doomed. Yet when we hear similar odds against a nuclear meltdown at Sellafield, we dismiss the idea as 'impossible'. It's flawed thinking like this that provides the bookies in town with a good living. There probably isn't a punter alive prepared to admit that he loses more money on the horses than he wins. So the bookies drive Jaguars, and maybe trade up to a newer model every couple of years, while their customers stand around waiting for the bus to come.

We don't have any bookmakers in Litterdale, so a man with money burning a hole in his pocket tends to gravitate towards the Fox, where the landlord combines his strenuous duties as a waterer of beer and purveyor of pork scratchings with the role of bookie's runner. There's racing on the telly every Saturday afternoon, and an open phone line to the bookies in town. The landlord has mounted the TV high on the wall. The regulars have to crane their necks to watch the 2.30 from Kempton, which helps to makes the beer go down quicker.

With the curtains pulled tight, to keep out the August sunshine, the Fox even feels like a bookies. The regulars scrutinise the racing pages, running stubby fingers down the columns of figures. It's like being an accountant, but doing it for fun. They know all about the runners and the riders, the favourites and the form. They all seem to have inside information (from the horse's mouth, perhaps?). With all these hot tips and dead certs being shared – conspiratorially, like playground secrets – it's hard to know why these guys don't win more often.

Actually, it's losing that they enjoy. They wouldn't admit it, of course, but it's true. Winning would create all sorts of problems: how to hide the money from their wives, for example, and how to avoid standing a celebratory round at the bar. Losing, in contrast, is a male bonding ritual that creates a warm feeling of comradeship. Everyone's in the same boat. Skint.

Anyone who reckons that men don't talk about their feelings should listen to a punter whose horse was way out in front ('twelve to one, it was... *twelve to one!*'), only for the nag to fall, inexplicably, at the very last fence. It's easier to blame life's disappointments on duff horses and useless jockeys than to confront their own shortcomings. If it costs a quid or two each week, isn't that better than just frittering their money away?

Anyone who doubts that life is, indeed, a lottery should try cycling. Those who take to two wheels know all there is to know about white-knuckle rides. Nobody gives way to cyclists, or 'organ donors' as they're known down at the A & E Department. Even when they take refuge in bus-lanes, they have to share them with taxis and buses: the cyclists' natural predators. A nasty accident is never more than a heartbeat away.

Cycling is an 'all or nothing' kind of deal these days. You can't just go for a bike ride any more; you have to buy into the whole cycling lifestyle. If you wear something sensible – a tweed jacket, perhaps, and a hat with ear-flaps – you'll be shunned by other cyclists. But if you wear what *they* wear (a helmet that looks like a pound of over-ripe bananas and figure-hugging Lycra in a variety of day-glo colours, embellished with a stripe of mud all the way up the back) you'll be openly mocked by everybody else. Prat or pariah, it's not an easy choice to make.

No wonder cyclists like to get out of town, and head for quiet Peakland lanes. Litterdale is a magnet for Lycra louts. Especially at this time of year, when sunny weekends encourage them to pedal out here, sit in a café where the tables and chairs are bolted to the floor, drink strong tea out of chipped mugs, and discuss the pressing matters of the day. No, just kidding, they talk about bikes. Of course.

✱